"You need to ge⟨…⟩
another day of ⟨…⟩
He put another piece of brush on the
fire. He continued to stand as if he
wasn't going to join her on the blanket.

"You aren't going to sleep?" Ellen asked.

"I think I'll sit up for a while."

"Then I'll keep you company—unless you've had enough of me?"

"I don't think that's possible," he said, and then a stricken look covered his features, as if he'd said something he hadn't meant to.

"We haven't had that talk yet," she said, just loud enough that she could be heard over the falls.

"Ellen, I don't think…"

"You're right. I don't want to talk." She stood. "I've spent the last two days worrying about dying."

"Ellen…"

She stepped around the fire. "There might not be another day, another time, and I want to celebrate being alive. With you."

Placing her hands on his shoulders, she went up on her toes and kissed him.

Chance grabbed her around the waist. Pulling her agains⟨…⟩ ⟨…⟩d.
His m⟨…⟩ ⟨…⟩a
banqu⟨…⟩

Dear Reader,

I love an adventure. And Ellen and Chance's story is just that. Take a fish-out-of-water female doctor, a man who has seen too much pain and can't do enough to help the people he cares deeply about, add a developing country, push the two doctors together, mix in drug traffickers chasing them and the fun begins.

I hope you enjoy Ellen and Chance's quest for love.

I want to thank Ron and Susie Woodward for sharing their experiences of working during medical mission trips in Central America. Because of their care many people like those I describe in my book now have better lives. You are both an inspiration to me.

I love to hear from my readers. You can reach me at SusanCarlisle.com.

Susan

THE DOCTOR'S SLEIGH BELL PROPOSAL

BY
SUSAN CARLISLE

Published in Great Britain 2016
By Mills & Boon, an imprint of HarperCollins*Publishers*
1 London Bridge Street, London, SE1 9GF

© 2016 Susan Carlisle

ISBN: 978-0-263-91529-7

Our policy is to use papers that are natural, renewable and recyclable products and made from wood grown in sustainable forests. The logging and manufacturing processes conform to the legal environmental regulations of the country of origin.

Printed and bound in Spain
by CPI, Barcelona

Susan Carlisle's love affair with books began in the sixth grade, when she made a bad grade in mathematics. Not allowed to watch TV until she'd brought the grade up, Susan filled her time with books. She turned her love of reading into a passion for writing, and now has over ten medical romances published through Mills & Boon. She writes about hot, sexy docs and the strong women who captivate them. Visit SusanCarlisle.com.

Books by Susan Carlisle

Mills & Boon Medical Romance

Midwives On-Call
His Best Friend's Baby

Heart of Mississippi
The Maverick Who Ruled Her Heart
The Doctor Who Made Her Love Again

Snowbound with Dr Delectable
The Rebel Doc Who Stole Her Heart
The Doctor's Redemption
One Night Before Christmas
Married for the Boss's Baby

Visit the Author Profile page at millsandboon.co.uk for more titles.

To Carol, I love you for being my sister—
if not by birth, of my heart.

CHAPTER ONE

SCREECHING VEHICLE BRAKES caught Dr. Chance Freeman's attention. That would be his three new staff members arriving. They should have been here last night but bad weather had delayed them. He'd needed them desperately. His other team had left that morning and today's clinic had been shorthanded and almost impossible to manage.

Chance glanced up from the baby Honduran boy he was examining and out the entrance of the canvas tent located in a clearing near a village. Beyond the long line of waiting patients, he saw a tall, twentyish woman jump down from the rear of the army surplus truck. She wore a tight green T-shirt, a bright yellow bandana round her neck and tan cargo pants that clung to her curves.

Great. High jungle fashion. He'd seen that before.

Shoulders hunched, he drew his lips into a tight line, stopping a long-suffering sound from escaping. Years ago he'd helped Alissa out of a Jeep. She'd believed in being well dressed in any environment as well. They had been newlyweds at the time. That had only lasted months.

Everything about this new staff member's regal bearing screamed she didn't belong in the stifling heat of a rain forest in Central America. He bet she wouldn't last long. In his years of doing medical aid work he'd learned to recognize those who would stick out the tough conditions and long hours. His guess was that she wasn't one of them. Everything about her screamed upper crust, big city. Pampered.

When had he become so cynical? He hadn't even met her yet and he was already putting her in a slot. It wasn't fair not to give her a chance just because she reminded him of his ex-wife. Still, he didn't have the time, energy or inclination to coddle anyone, even if he desperately needed the help.

From under her wide-brimmed hat she scanned the area, her gaze coming around to lock with his. She tilted her head, shielding her eyes with a hand against the noon-day sun. One of her two companions said something and she turned away.

Shaking off the spell, Chance returned to the child. He'd hardly looked down when there was a commotion outside. People were screaming and running. *What was going on?*

He didn't have to wait long to find out. Two men carried another man into the tent. He was bleeding profusely around the face and neck area and down one arm. Quickly handing the baby to his mother, Chance cleared the exam table with his arm.

"Put him here. What happened?"

The men lifted the injured man onto the table. Despite Chance's excellent Spanish, they were talking so fast he was having to work to understand them. Apparently, the man had been attacked by a jaguar while trying to save one of his goats.

A feminine voice asked from the end of the table, "What can I do to help?"

A fragrant scent floated in the air. He was tempted to lean forward and inhale. There was a marked difference between the feminine whiff and the odor of the sweaty bodies around him. Unfortunately, he would need to warn her not to wear perfume in this part of the world because it attracted unwanted insects.

Chance looked up into clear blue eyes that made him think of the pool of water at the bottom of his favorite waterfall. The woman he'd just seen climbing off the truck waited. She'd removed her hat and now he could clearly see a long blonde braid falling over a shoulder. With her fair coloring she would burn in no time in the hot Honduran sun.

"Start with cutting away the clothing."

She stepped to the table. The paper on the table was soaked with blood. He glanced up to see her face blanch as she viewed the man who would be disfigured for life from the deep lacerations.

"Don't faint on me," Chance said through clenched teeth. "Michael, get over here." He nodded toward the other table. "Go help there. Michael and I'll handle this."

She moved off to see about the case Michael was working on. Chance didn't have time to ponder why someone in the medical profession couldn't handle this type of injury.

He and Michael worked to piece the Honduran man back together. It may have been the largest number of stitches he'd ever put into a person. There would be a long recovery time.

"We need some help here," Michael called as he finished suturing an area.

The woman stepped to the table again.

Chance glared at her. "I thought I told you—"

She gave him a determined and unwavering look. "I've got this." She turned to Michael. "What do you need?"

"Bandage this hand," he said.

"I'll take care of it." The words were full of confidence as fingers tipped in hot pink picked up the saline and four-by-fours sitting on the table and began cleaning around the area.

Chance had to stop himself from rolling his eyes. That manicure wouldn't last long here and there wouldn't be another forthcoming either. He moved on to the next laceration. As he looked at the man's arm Chance kept a watchful eye on the new staff member. With the efficiency of few he'd seen, she'd wrapped and secured the dressing and moved on the next spot.

At least she seemed to have recovered from whatever her earlier issue had been. He was used to temporary help, but he still wanted quality.

Many who came to help with the Traveling Clinic were filled with good intentions and the idealism of saving the world but didn't have the skills or common sense required to work in such primitive settings. The clinic served the medical issues in the small villages outside of La Ceiba. Making it even more difficult was that the locals were often hesitant about asking for help.

A jaguar attack wasn't the clinic's normal kind of injury but they did see a number of severe wounds from accidents. He needed staff that could handle the unexpected and often gruesome. If Chance wasn't such a sceptic he'd have given the new woman points for her recovery but he'd been doing this type of work for far too long. Had seen staff come and go.

He was familiar with people who left. His mother had done it when he'd been a child. He'd been seven when she'd just not been there. His father was a world-renowned surgeon and had been gone much of the time. With his mother's absence Chance had starting acting out in an effort to keep his father's attention, even to the point of stealing. That had got him sent to boarding school. Even in that restrictive environment Chance had pushed back.

In a stern voice the headmaster had said, "It's time for

you to decide if you're going to amount to anything in your life. Right now I'd be surprised if you do."

He was the one man in Chance's life who had taken a real interest in a scared and angry boy. The grizzled and gruff headmaster had believed in him, had taken time to listen. Unlike his father. Chance had wanted to make the headmaster proud and had made a change after that conversation. He'd focused on his studies. Dedicated his life to helping others. But in the area of personal relationships he had failed miserably over and over to the point he had long ago given up. Those, apparently, he wasn't capable of having.

Why were dark memories invading now? Maybe because the new woman reminded him so much of his ex-wife, Alissa, whose defection always made him think of his mother. Two females who had rejected him. He'd moved past all that long ago. His worry now was how to keep the clinic open. Pondering old history did nothing to help with the present problem.

He watched the new woman as he changed gloves. Her movements were confident now. Marco, a local man who served as clerk, translator, and gofer for the clinic, entered the tent with a distressed look on his face. He hurried to her and said in his heavily accented voice, "I know not where you are. Please not leave again without telling. Much danger here. Not get lost."

She looked at him. "I'm sorry. I saw the emergency and thought I should come help."

"It's okay, Marco. I'll explain. See to the other two," Chance said to the short, sturdy man.

"*Sí*, Dr. Chance." Marco nodded and hurried out of the clinic.

Chance gave her a pointed look. "Please don't leave the clinic area until we've talked."

Her chin went down and she nodded. "I understand.

By the way, my name is Cox. Dr. Ellen Cox. Like Bond. James Bond." She flashed him a grin.

She was a cheeky little thing. He wasn't certain he appreciated that.

He finished up with the injured man and sent him off in a truck to the hospital in La Ceiba. He would check in on him when they got back to town. Chance cleaned up and moved on to his next patient, who was an older woman with an infected bug bite. It would be necessary to drain it.

Before starting the procedure, he stepped to the table next to his, where a five-year-old girl sat. Digging into his pants pocket, he pulled out a peppermint and handed the piece of candy to her. She removed the clear plastic cover and plopped it into her mouth, giving Chance a wide, toothy grin. He'd given a child a second of happiness. He just wished he could make more of a difference. What he did wasn't enough.

As Chance returned to his patient, Ellen joined him.

Since she was so enthusiastic he'd let her see to the woman as he watched. "We're going to need a suture kit, a box of four-by-fours and bandages. Supplies are in the van." He gestured toward the beat-up vehicle that had been parked partially under the tent so that the back end was protected from the daily afternoon rain and could function as a portable storage room. Chance waited as she hurried after the supplies.

Returning to his side, she placed the kit on the bed and a bottle of saline water as well. "I'll get a pan." She was gone again.

Chance spoke to his patient in Spanish, reassuring her that she would be fine and that what he was going to do wouldn't take too long. A few moments later Ellen was back with the pan and plastic gloves for herself.

He helped the older woman lay back on the table.

Ellen gave the patient a reassuring pat on the shoulder and then turned her attention to opening the suture kit, placing it where he could easily reach the contents. Taking the plastic gloves off the top, he pulled them on. She did the same with hers. Removing the blue sterile paper sheets, she placed them on her patient's leg around and under the inflamed area.

Chance handed her the scalpel. She took it without question.

Michael called, "Chance, you got a second to look at this?"

"Go ahead. I can handle this," Ellen said.

Chance hesitated then nodded. He liked to oversee the new staff for a week or so just to make sure they understood the locals and the type of work they were doing but she should be able to handle a simple case.

The patient's eyes had grown wide when he'd left. Ellen moved to his side of the table and began speaking to her in a mix that was more English than Spanish. As she distracted the woman by having her pay attention to what she was saying instead of what she was doing, the woman calmed down to the point of smiling a few times.

Chance glanced Ellen's way now and then to see how she was doing. By the time he returned the patient was bandaged and ready to leave. Ellen had done a good job.

Chance moved on to the next person waiting. She assisted him. They were just finishing when Marco returned with the two other new staff members. He introduced the man as Pete Ortiz and the woman as Karen Johnson, both nurses. Ellen moved off across the short aisle of tables to help Chance's colleague, Michael Lange. Because Pete spoke fluent Spanish, Chance sent him to do triage and Karen stayed to help him.

Working in Honduras on and off for eight years had

only made Chance see the needs here grow. There had been a time he'd thought he might really make a difference but the people needed real clinics, brick-and-mortar buildings with dedicated doctors, not just a few coming in and out every few weeks.

He loved this country—the weather, which he much preferred to the cold of the north, the coast. Scuba diving was one of his greatest day-off hobbies. Walking through a rain forest and being surprised by a waterfall was amazing. But most of all he liked the open, generous smiles of the people. In Honduras he had found home.

The Traveling Clinic had been his idea years ago and he'd worked long and hard to gain funding for the idea. The clinic was a successful concept but money was forever a problem. Again tomorrow the clinic would be stopping at a different village and the locals would line up. Some would wait all day for care. The day would start just as this one had. Never enough, and more left to do.

A couple of times during the afternoon hours the sound of laughter reached his ears. Michael and the new doctor seemed to enjoy working together. That was what he'd thought when his wife had spent so much time helping his clinic colleague, Jim. They had gotten along so well she'd returned to the States with him.

The sun was only touching the tops of the trees by the time Chance saw his last patient. Michael was finishing up with his as well. Now all that was left was to break down the clinic, load the trucks, and head for a hot shower. He leaned up against the nearest exam table, finishing a note on his patient's chart.

"Doctor, if you'll excuse me, I need to fold this exam table." Ellen gave him a pointed look as she flipped her hair back, implying he needed to move.

She reminded him of a teenager, looked no older than a fresh-out-of-high-school girl, even though she must be at least twenty-eight to his tired forty-one-year-old eyes. Breaking down the clinic was the job of Marco and the local men he'd hired to help him. As much as Chance was amazed by her zeal, she needed to understand a few things about the culture and dangers here. "Marco and his men will take care of that."

"I can get—"

He lowered his voice. "I'm sure you can but they take their jobs and positions seriously. I don't want them to feel insulted."

"Oh. I didn't realize." She stopped what she was doing.

"Now you do. You need to tread more carefully, Dr. Cox. There are cultural and safety issues you should be aware of before you go off willy-nilly. Don't be reckless. This isn't Los Angeles, New York or wherever you are from."

A flash of something in her eyes he couldn't put a name to came and went before she said, "New York."

He looked at her a second. "There're not only animals in the jungle that could hurt you, as you saw today, but there's a major issue with drug traders. Neither play around or allow second chances. You should never go out alone. Even in the villages or clinic compound, always have someone with you."

"Are you trying to scare me?"

Did she think this was some exotic vacation spot? "No, I'm trying to keep you out of harm's way." He looked straight at her. "If you don't follow the rules, you don't stay around here long."

Her lips tightened as she glanced toward the men working to break down the clinic. "I'm sorry I upset Marco. I saw the number of people waiting and thought I should get to work."

"You would be no good to them if you get hurt."

"Your point is taken."

"Chance," Michael called.

"Just remember what I said." He walked away to join Michael beside the supply van.

Half an hour later the tent was down and everything stowed in the vehicles. Now their party was bumping along the narrow dirt road toward the coast. Chance rode in the supply van, with one of the locals driving, while Michael was a passenger in the truck. The others rode in the rear of it. The hour-long trip to the resort might be the toughest part of the day. As the bird flew, the distance wasn't far; however, the roads were so rough and winding it seemed to take forever to make the return drive. Chance usually tried to sleep.

For some reason his thoughts went to the young doctor traveling in the truck behind him. She'd worked hard, doing her share and some more. There was no way she was napping while sitting on that hard metal bench. If she complained, he would point out that the ride was just part of doing this type of medical work. Anyone who stayed with it learned to accept the hardship.

Ellen's head bumped against one of the support frames running around the bed of the truck. Taking a nap was almost impossible. She pulled a jacket out of her duffel bag and folded it up then stuffed it between her head and the unforgiving metal.

Looking out through the slats, she watched the fascinating countryside go by. The vegetation grew rich and huge. Some of the leaves were the size of an umbrella. And so green. It looked impossible to walk through. She'd never seen anything like it. The flowers were such vivid colors. A pink hibiscus always caught her attention.

As the plane had been coming in that morning she'd looked down on the coastline of the county. The pristine white sand against the blue-green of the water had made her want to experience it for herself. It was a beautiful country. She already loved it.

Completely different from New York, the city of buildings and lights. She'd worked at an inner-city clinic that saw pregnant teenagers and babies with colds. It was nothing compared to the type of patients and conditions she'd experienced today. It had been exhilarating. Except for that one moment when she'd looked at that man and all the memories of her mother caught in the car had come flooding back.

The Traveling Clinic cared for people who truly needed it. These people had no other way of getting medical care. They hadn't made poor life choices like the drug addicts and drunks in the city. Here they had nothing, and the clinic offered them something they desperately needed. And they still had a bright smile to share.

The type of work she'd done today was why she'd become a doctor. As a child, a car accident had killed her mother and had left Ellen in the hospital for weeks. There she'd learned the importance of good medical care. The staff had loved and given special attention to the little girl who had lost so much. Ellen had determined then that she wanted to work in the medical field, do for people what had been done for her.

The only sticking point had been her father. As a Manhattan socialite and the only child of an overprotective father, she'd worked at being taken seriously when she'd announced she was going to medical school. Ellen desired to do more than chair committees and plan fancy fund-raisers. She'd wanted to personally make a difference, get to know the people she was helping.

When Ellen had started practicing at the inner-city clinic her father had pitched a fit, saying it was too risky and he didn't want her to work there.

"You're acting like your mother. She went in head first

and then thought," he'd said more than once to her as she'd been growing up.

Ellen had told him he had no choice. A number of times she'd noticed a man hanging around when she'd come and gone from the clinic. Some days later she'd found out he had been hired by her father to watch over her because he'd been concerned about her safety.

A few weeks later she'd heard Dr. Freeman speak with such passion about his work in Honduras that she had been hooked. She wanted to make that kind of difference, offer that kind of care. The next day she'd applied to join his staff. It had taken her six months but she was finally here.

After her decision to come to Honduras, she'd thought of not telling her father but she loved him too much to just disappear. Instead, she'd told him she was going to Honduras but not specifically where she would be, fearing he'd send someone to watch over her. Again he'd accused her of not thinking it through. She'd assured him she had. For once she wanted to do something on her own, free from her father's influence.

Her head bounced again. The picture of Dr. Freeman's displeased look when she'd frozen came to mind. Her lips formed a wry smile. Later she had seen a small measure of respect in his eyes.

The wheels squealed to a painful halt. Ellen looked out the end of the truck to see a gorgeously groomed area. Where were they? The others filed off the vehicle and she brought up the rear. With her feet on the ground, she looked around. It appeared as if they were in the back parking lot of a resort.

A couple of Honduran helpers pulled her bag, along with Pete's and Karen's, down from the truck. She hadn't met her fellow staff members until the time had come to board the flight to Honduras. Pete was a nice guy who was looking for a change after a bad marriage and Karen was a middle-aged woman who thought working with the clinic would be a nice way to see a new country. Ellen had liked them both immediately.

Their group was joined by the two doctors. She'd enjoyed working with Michael Lange. He seemed fun and laid back. The same couldn't be said about Dr. Freeman. From what she could tell, he was an excellent doctor. Everything she'd heard about him had been glowing. But on the Mr. Congeniality scale he was pretty low. He could work on his warm welcomes. He hadn't even taken the time to offer his name.

After hearing him speak Ellen had expected him to have less of a crusty personality. He acted as if he'd seen too much and couldn't leave it behind. He was as strikingly handsome as she remembered. With thick, dark, wavy hair with a touch of white at the temples that gave him an air of authority, he was someone who held her attention. Even when she hadn't been working directly with him she had been conscious of where he'd been in the tent. She generally didn't have this type of reaction to a man.

"I'll show Ellen to her hut," Michael said.

"No, she's next to me," Chance said. "You see to, uh, Pete and…" He looked at the other nurse. "It's Karen, isn't it?"

"That's correct." Karen picked up her bag.

"Okay. Dinner is at seven in the private dining room behind the main one." Dr. Freeman headed toward a dirt path between two low palmetto plants. There was a small wooden sign there giving arrowed directions to different areas of the resort. "Coming, Dr. Cox? I've got a call to make to the States before it gets too late."

He'd not offered to carry her luggage. If he thought she couldn't or wouldn't carry her own bag, he had another thought coming. Grabbing her duffel, she pulled the strap over her shoulder and hurried after him. The man really was egotistical.

She followed him along a curving path through groomed vegetation beneath trees filled with blue and yellow chattering macaws. She lagged behind when she became caught up in her surroundings. The place was jaw-dropping beautiful. Completely different from any place she'd ever seen.

"Dr. Cox." The exasperation in the doctor's voice reminded her of a father talking to a distracted child. She didn't like it.

"It's Ellen."

"Come along, *Ellen*. I still have work to do tonight." He took long strides forward.

From what she could tell, he had more than put in a day's worth of work. What could he possibly need to do tonight? "Coming, sir."

He stopped and glared down his nose at her. "The *sir* isn't necessary."

"I just thought that since you were acting like a general I should speak to you as such."

"Ellen, you'll find I'm not known for my sense of humor." He continued on down the path as if he didn't care if she followed him or not.

"I'm sure you're not," she murmured. Hefting her bag strap more securely over her shoulder, she focused on catching up. They moved farther into the landscape until they came out in a small grassy opening where two huts stood with only a huge banyan tree separating them. Each had a thatched roof and a dark-stained wooden porch with what looked like comfortable chairs with bright floral pillows.

The space was perfect as a romantic getaway. "This is amazing. I expected to live in a tent and have to use a bathhouse."

"You have a top-of-the-line bath. We work hard and the board believes the least it can do is provide a nice place to stay. The resort gives us a deal." Dr. Freeman pointed to the structure on the left. "That hut is yours. Follow the signs around to the dining room. If you need something, call zero on the phone." With that he headed toward the other hut.

Well, she wouldn't be counting on him to be the perfect neighbor.

Ellen climbed the three steps to the main door. There was a hammock hanging from one post to another. The living arrangements weren't what she'd expected but she wasn't going to complain.

She swung the door open and entered. Her eyes widened. She sucked in a breath of pleasure. Talk about going from one extreme to another. As rough as the working conditions were, the living quarters were luxurious. She'd lived well in New York but even by those standards this was a nice living space.

The floor plan consisted of an open room with a sitting area on one side and the bed on the other. The ceiling was high with a slow-moving fan that encouraged a breeze through the slated windows. A gleaming wood floor stretched the length of the room. The only area of it that was covered was in the sitting area, where two chairs and a settee created a cozy group. A large bright rug of red, greens and yellows punctuated the space.

But it was the bedroom side that made the biggest impression. A large square canopy bed made of mahogany with identical twists carved into each of the four posts sat there. If she was going to spend a honeymoon somewhere, this would be her choice.

She'd come close to a wedding a couple of times but it seemed like her father stepped in and changed her mind just as she was getting serious. It was as if he couldn't trust her to know who and what she wanted. That was one of the reasons she'd come to Honduras. At least here she could make her own decisions.

The open-air shower, shielded from any onlookers by plank walls, was a new experience. At first she found it intimidating but as the warm water hit her shoulders Ellen eased into the enjoyment of the birds in the trees chirping at her. She was officially enchanted.

Half an hour later, Ellen headed down the plant-lined walk in the direction of what she hoped was the dining area. She turned a curve and a crystal-blue swimming pool that resembled a fern-encircled grotto came into view. The resort was truly amazing.

Beside it Dr. Freeman sat on a lounger, talking on the phone. He wore a T-shirt, cargo shorts and leather thong shoes. His legs were crossed at the ankles. He appeared relaxed but the tone of his voice said that was far from the case. She wasn't surprised. Her impression had been that he didn't unwind often.

"Look, we need those supplies. We have to raise the money." He paused. "I can't be in two places at once. You'll have to handle it. And about the staff you're sending me, I've got to have people who'll stay longer than six weeks. No more short term. The people of rural Honduras need a standing clinic." He glanced in her direction.

Ellen continued toward a tall open-air building, hoping it was where she should go. Footfalls followed her.

"Eavesdropping, Dr. Cox?"

She looked back at him. "I wasn't. I was just on my way to dinner. And I told you I prefer Ellen. When you say Dr. Cox it sounds so condescending."

"I'm sorry. *Ellen.*"

She now wished she hadn't insisted he call her by her first name. His slight accent gave it an exotic note that sent a shiver up her spine. Not wanting to give that reaction any more analysis, she said, "I'm hungry."

"The dining room is this way." He started up the steps to the building and she joined him.

They entered a large open space with a thatched roof supported by huge poles. A wooden desk with a local man standing behind it was located off to one side. He waved in their direction as they crossed the gleaming wooden floor. Ellen followed him around one of three groupings of wicker furniture toward a shuttered doorway that stood open. Inside were tables with white cloths over them and low lighting. Dr. Freeman kept moving then stopped at a single door and opened it.

"Close the door behind you," he instructed.

Ellen did as he asked. They were now in a small room where a long table was set in the middle and a buffet area along one wall. The other members of their group were already there, talking among themselves. They grew quiet as she and Dr. Freeman joined them.

"I thought you guys would already be eating."

"Not without you, boss," Michael said with a grin.

"You know better than that. Well, if no one else is going to start, I am." Dr. Freeman picked up a plate off the stack on the buffet table. Everyone else followed his lead and lined up. Unsure of the protocol or the seating arrangement, Ellen moved to the back of the line. A minute or two later, with her plate full of chicken and tropical fruit, she considered which chair to take.

"Come and sit beside me," Michael offered.

With a smile Ellen took the open seat. She glanced at Chance. His eyes narrowed as he looked in their direction.

She and Michael discussed where she was from and what she thought of her hut then he asked, "So, Ellen, what brings you to our little slice of the world?"

She shrugged. "I wanted to work where I could make a difference."

"You weren't doing that where you were?" Dr. Freeman asked.

She hadn't realized he'd been listening to their conversation.

"Yes, but these people really need someone here. I was seeing young mothers and babies. I found my job necessary and rewarding but there was a tug to do something more. Others were there to help those girls but not enough here to help these. I wanted to come here."

"How did you find out about us?" Michael asked.

"I heard Dr. Freeman speak. I knew this was where I wanted to be."

"Well, Chance, you made a convert."

Dr. Freeman shrugged and went back to eating.

"So, what did you think about the work today?" Michael asked.

"It was different, I have to give you that. But I loved it." She glanced toward the end of the table where Dr. Freeman was sitting.

"You might feel differently after a few days of hot, unending work," Dr. Freeman drawled.

"Aw, come on, Chance, don't scare her." Michael smiled at her. "Don't worry about him. The great Chance Freeman has seen so many people come and go here he's a little cynical about all the new ones. Many don't stay the full six weeks. Some have only lasted days. It's made him a little jaded."

"That's enough, Michael."

The doctor's snap didn't seem to faze Michael. He just grinned. Ellen looked at Dr. Freeman. "I don't plan to be leaving anytime soon, Dr. Freeman."

"Dr. Freeman?" Michael chuckled. "We're a casual

bunch around here. First names work just fine. Especially after hours. Isn't that right, Chance?"

He leaned back in his chair. "Sure."

After that Michael turned his attention to Pete and Karen, asking them about themselves.

Ellen concentrated on her dinner and was glad to have Dr. Freeman…uh, Chance's attention off her. When everyone had finished laughing at a story Michael told, Chance tapped on the table with the back of his fork to gain their attention.

"Okay, we need to talk about tomorrow. We'll be in the Tooca area. Near the river. This is our first time there so let's be on our toes. We'll need to be at the trucks at four a.m., ready to roll. Get some sleep and be ready for a really long day."

Ellen shuffled out of the dining room with the rest of the group. It turned out that Karen was housed not far from her so they walked back toward their huts together. After leaving Karen, Ellen continued along the path lit only by lights in the vegetation. Thankfully the porch lights were on at her and Chance's huts. One of the staff at the resort must have come by while she'd been at dinner.

Ellen had just crawled under the covers when the light flicked on inside Chance's hut. His silhouette crossed in front of the window. His passion for what he did was a major factor in why she'd come to Honduras. It was obvious he needed nurses and doctors to help him. So what was his problem with welcoming her?

CHAPTER TWO

THE SUN WAS SLOWLY topping the nearest palm tree when the caravan of three vehicles pulled into a clearing near the River Sico. Chance climbed out of the Jeep that had been leading the caravan and walked over to speak to the local village leader, who was there to greet him. Returning to his staff, who were already beginning to set up the tent, he searched for Ellen. To his surprise she was all smiles and asking what she could do to help. The early hour didn't seem to bother her. Did nothing faze the woman?

She'd traveled for over ten hours the day before, put in five hours of work, and had had to wake up at four a.m. and ride in the back of an uncomfortable truck, and she was still chipper. He was afraid her fall would be hard. No one could keep up that positive attitude for long.

Still, he was having a hard time not liking her. And she was certainly nice to look at. Too much so.

Marco and his crew had the tent erected in no time and were working on setting up tables as Chance directed the van driver into place.

Ellen came to stand beside him. "Good morning. Michael said I should see you about my duties."

"Did you sleep well?"

Her brows drew together as if she was unsure of his motive for asking. "Actually, I did. Thanks for asking."

"You're going to need that rest because we have a long, full day ahead of us. We all kind of do what's needed when needed. The lines are blurred between the doctors and nurses here. So you'll know what supplies we have and where they are stored. Why don't you supply each station with bandages, suture kits, saline bottles and antiseptic? Any basic working supplies you are familiar with."

"Will do."

"Under no circumstances do you open the locked box behind the seat of the van without permission. There's a prevalent drug problem here and we have to be careful drugs are not stolen. There's only one key and I have it. If you need something you must see me."

"I understand."

"When you're finished putting out supplies you'll be needed to work triage. People are already lining up."

A steady stream of patients entered the tent over the next four hours. Karen worked with him and she seemed comfortable with all he'd asked her to do. He'd had little time to check on Ellen. When he had, she'd been either leaning over, intently listening to a patient, or in a squatting position, speaking to the mother of a child.

At noon the patients dwindled to nothing. Chance stepped outside the tent, hoping for a breeze. Ellen walked toward him.

"Are we done here?"

Chance let out a dry chuckle and waved his hand to discourage a fly. "Not by a long shot. Everyone stops for lunch. We'll start over with twice the number in an hour. Marco should have our food ready. Get something to eat and drink then take a moment to rest."

With the back of her hand Ellen pushed away the strand

of hair sticking to her forehead. Some of it remained and Chance was tempted to reach out and help her. He resisted the urge. Getting involved on a personal level even with something as benign as moving her hair wasn't going to happen.

"You can wash up behind the tent. Remember what I said about not straying from the area." He turned and walked off toward Michael, who had just exited the clinic. Watching out of the corner of his eye, he saw Ellen headed round the tent.

"The new crew is really working out," Michael said when Chance reached him.

"Yeah."

"Ellen seems especially capable."

"She won't last long."

"Why? Because she's blonde and beautiful?" Michael said drily.

"That has nothing to do with it."

"Sure it does. They aren't all Alissa. I have a feeling this one might surprise you."

Chance huffed. "It won't matter. She'll do her six weeks and we'll have to train someone else. Just see to it you don't get too attached."

Michael grinned and raised his brows. "Me? Get attached? But there's nothing wrong with a little fun."

"Just don't let it affect the clinic work." Michael was a good guy but Chance didn't need any personal relationship getting in the way of work. He knew first-hand how emotional upheaval could make the working situation difficult. It had been his own issue with his wife and the affair that she had been having with his colleague that had done it last time. He'd lost all the staff and had almost had to give up the clinic altogether. The only way he had survived had been to push forward and devote all his off time to finding new funding for the clinic.

"Have I ever?" Michael said, his grin growing to a smile.

They both knew it had. Michael was known for show-ing the young female members a good time while they were in Honduras. For some reason Chance didn't like the idea of him doing so with Ellen. "Let's get some lunch before patients start lining up again. I noticed they are coming in by the canoe load now. In the future we need to think about setting up near rivers so that more people will have access."

Michael's look sobered. "We need to think about where we're going to get some major support so that we can build a permanent building to work out of."

"I know. I'm going to have to go to the States soon and start doing some fund-raising." Chance didn't like the dog and pony show he seemed to have to put on for all the wealthy potential donors to get money but un-derstood the necessity. Give them a good time and they would give was the motto. Still, it was so little in the face of so much need.

Sympathy filled Michael's voice. "But you hate the idea."

"I'm more about the work and less about begging for money."

"Maybe it's time to find someone who'll handle fun-draising full time."

Chance had tried before but nothing had worked out. "I need to check on a couple of things and I'll get lunch." Michael headed round the tent and Chance entered the clinic to find Ellen replenishing supplies. "What're you doing? I thought I told you to get some lunch and rest."

"Marco didn't have everything set out yet so I came to check on the supplies and get things ready for this af-ternoon."

"I appreciate what you're doing but I've seen people burn out pretty quickly here."

She looked at him. "Doctor, I can assure you that I am nowhere near being burned out."

"It sneaks up on you."

For a moment she gave him a speculative look. "Is that what has happened to you?"

The statement seared him. "What do you mean?"

"You seem to care about these people but at the same time don't welcome the people who come to help you. You've been trying to run me off from the minute I got here."

Anger rose in him. Was he letting the past boil over that much? "I have not. There's not enough help as it is. Why would I discourage anyone?"

"I'm wondering the same thing."

"I want you to know the facts. And you don't seem the type cut out for this kind of work."

"And you have decided this by…" she cocked her head "…the clothes I wear, the color of my eyes, my shoes?"

"Your age. Your looks. You attitude. In my experience someone like you only comes to a place like this as a lark, running from something, looking for adventure or to prove something." She flinched. So he had touched a nerve. What had brought her here?

"Why, Dr. Freeman, I do believe you're a bigot. And it must be nice to be all-knowing. It doesn't matter what you think. The real question is have you had any problems with the work I have done so far?"

She had a way of cutting to the point. He hadn't. In fact, he'd been surprised at her knowledge and efficiency. He said nothing.

"That's what I thought. Now, if you don't mind, I'll get that lunch you think I need so badly." She stalked out of the tent.

Wow, there might be more to the blonde bombshell than he'd given her credit for. Had he really been that tough on her? Unfair? She had certainly stood up to him. Been a capable doctor. Maybe he should cut her some slack.

By the time Chance had made it to the lunch table Ellen was finished with her meal and headed toward the front of the clinic. "Remember not to go out of sight of the clinic or one of us."

"I'll heed your warning, Doctor," she said in a sarcastic tone as she kept moving, not giving him time to respond.

Despite what she said, it didn't ease his concern. He felt responsible for all his staff but for some reason Ellen seemed so naive that she required more attention. A couple of times the new people hadn't taken his warnings seriously and had almost gotten in trouble. He couldn't let that happen to her.

He returned to the front and took a seat on a stool just inside the tent door. Ellen was sitting on a blanket she'd apparently taken from the supply van. Chance tried not to appear as if he was watching but she claimed his attention. As she sat, a few of the village girls approached. Ellen spoke to them in a soft voice, halting a couple of times as if searching for the correct word. One of the girls tentatively picked up Ellen's hand and touched her fingernail.

"You like my polish?" Ellen smiled and held her fingers out wide.

The child nodded and the other girls stepped closer, each stroking a nail in wonder.

"Stay here and I'll be right back." Gracefully she rose and headed for the transport truck as if on a mission. She climbed onto the back bumper and reached in to pull out a backpack. Looking through a side pocket, she removed a small bottle. After dropping the bag back into the truck, she returned to the girls. Ellen sat and the children gathered around her again. She patted the blanket and invited them to join her, then opened the bottle. Taking one of the girls' hands, Ellen placed it on her bent knee and applied polish to a nail. There was a unified sound of awe.

What the hell? The woman had brought fingernail polish into the jungle.

Bright smiles formed on dark faces. Small bodies shifted closer in an effort to have a turn. Ellen had their complete attention. Her blonde head contrasted against those around her. The girls giggled and admired their nails, showing them off to their friends before jumping up and running to display them for someone else. As one left another joined Ellen.

Her mirth mingled with the children's. The sound was unusual in the rain forest yet seemed to belong. Like the sweet song of birds in the trees.

Chance walked toward her. It was time to get started again or patients would go unseen and he couldn't let that happen. He stood over the little group. "You seem to have created a stir."

Ellen looked at him with a grin on her face and moved to stand. "Every female likes to do a little something special for herself."

She wobbled and Chance reached for her elbow, helping her to stand. A shot of awareness he'd not felt in years went through him. It was both exciting and disturbing. To cover his reaction he said, "Even if they can't have it all the time."

Ellen glared at him. "Especially then. A moment of pleasure is better than none."

What would it be like to share pleasure with her? Whoa, had the noon sun gone to his head? That wasn't something he should be thinking about in regard to any of his staff and certainly not about this too young, too idealistic newcomer. Life had taught him that picking women wasn't his strong suit.

Chance released her arm as if it had turned into a hot

coal. "I'll see you in the clinic. You'll be working with Michael this afternoon until I think you know the ropes well enough to handle cases on your own."

Ellen didn't know what had gotten into Chance but she was relieved that she didn't have to assist him. Working with Michael was easy and fun so why did it seem anticlimactic next to helping Chance? There was an intriguing intensity about him that tugged at her.

He had seemed so much larger than life when she'd heard him speak. The passion and compassion he felt for the people of Honduras had vibrated through her with each of his words. She'd been drawn to this place. But she'd fought too long and too hard to make her own decisions and Chance was too bossy for her taste. She didn't need another man overseeing her life.

One of the girls who'd had her nails done was Chance's patient at the next table. Despite having her back to them, Ellen overheard him say, "Your nails are so pretty."

She smiled. Mr. Gruff and Groan might have a heart after all.

During the rest of the afternoon and into the dimming light of evening came the continuing blur of people with open wounds, bug bites, sores, to serious birth defects. Thunder rolled in the distance and the wind whipped the tent as the last of the patients were being seen.

"Get started on putting things away. We need to get on the road before this hits," Chance called to everyone as he finished cleaning a wound on the calf of his last patient, a middle-aged man.

Ellen began storing the supplies in the van. As she passed by Chance he said, "Ellen, would you get an antibiotic out of the med cabinet for me?" He held up a key attached to a ring.

"Sure." Her hand brushed his larger one as she took it. A tingle went through her. Why this reaction to him of all people? She wasn't looking for that. Hadn't come here expecting it. She hurried toward the van.

Entering the vehicle, she made her way down the small isle to where the med box was located. Constructed of metal and bolted to the floor for security, it was situated behind the bench seat. She went down on her knees in front of it. The light was so poor she fumbled with the key in the lock. Slipping her hand into the side leg pocket of her cargo pants, she pulled out her penlight. She balanced it on a nearby shelf, directing the beam toward the lock.

The screech of the driver's door opening drew her attention. She glanced over her shoulder. A thin young man held a knife in her direction. Fear made her heart pound. Her hand holding the lock shook. She opened her mouth to scream.

The man leaned over the seat bring the knife to her neck. *"Tranquillo."*

Ellen remained quiet as he'd asked. She glanced out the end of the van. What was she going to do? She couldn't give him the meds and she had to protect the others.

The tip of the knife was pushed against her skin. The man hovered over her. He smelled of sweat and wet clothes.

"What do you want?" she asked.

"The drugs," the man bit out. "Open the box."

The urgent demand in his voice told her he meant business. When she didn't immediately move he pressed the knife against her and growled, "Now."

Panic welled in her. She couldn't give him the drugs but the blade at her neck reminded her that she couldn't put him off long either.

With relief and renewed alarm she heard Chance call, "Ellen?"

"Say no word," the man whispered, slipping down behind the seat but still holding the knife to her neck.

She had to warn Chance.

Why hadn't Ellen returned? Chance headed toward the van.

He had finished applying the bandage around the man's leg. All he needed to do now was give him the antibiotics and they could get on the road. A commotion outside caught his attention. A young man who looked like he was in his twenties was being helped into the tent by another Honduran about the same age. There was a rag soaked in blood on his arm. Michael and Karen were aiding them. Marco and one of his men had started setting up the exam table they had just folded. They could handle the situation. He wanted to know what Ellen was doing.

He instructed his patient to remain where he was. The rear of the van had been driven under the back of the tent. The area was shadowy because the portable lamps were being used around the exam tables. With the dimming light of the day, compounded by the storm, it was hard to see.

As Chance neared the open doors he saw the small glow of what must be Ellen's penlight. "Hey, what's taking you so long?"

She was on her knees on the floor, facing the medicine box. Her head turned slowly toward him. Even in the disappearing light Chance could see the fear in her eyes. She looked as if she was imploring him to leave. There was a slight movement behind her. Ellen shook her head almost imperceptibly.

Chance kept eye contact and nodded. "Hurry up, I need those meds."

"Yes, sir."

Sir? She knew he didn't like being called sir. Something was definitely wrong.

He backed away from the van. The others were still busy with the injured patient. Rushing past them and outside, he started round the tent when he met Marco. In a low voice he told him that Ellen was in trouble and to give him to the count of ten then run inside the clinic, hollering for help. Marco nodded and Chance circled the outside of the tent until he could see the driver's side van door. It stood open. He could make out the outline of a man in the seat with his back to the door and one leg on the running board. Dread seized him. The man must have a weapon on Ellen.

Giving thanks for the storm brewing, which would cover any noise he made, Chance moved out to the edge of the clearing and followed it around until he was facing the front of the van. When the thunder rolled again Chance ran as fast as he could and slammed his body into the door. The man let out a startled yelp and twisted in the seat, reaching for his leg. Chance grabbed the door and swung it hard again. This time it hit the man in the head and he dropped to the ground, along with a knife.

"Ellen!" Chance barked. "Ellen, are you okay?"

"I'm fine." She sounded shaken.

Marco joined him. Chance left him to tie the vandal up while he climbed into the van. Looking over the seat, he saw Ellen still sitting on the floor, with her head in her hands. "Are you hurt?"

She said nothing.

He reached out and placed a hand on her shoulder. "Ellen, are you hurt? Did he cut you?"

Slowly she looked up. "No." She held up his keys. "And I didn't let him get any drugs. Do I get atta-girl points?"

"Hell, woman, I'd rather he'd had all the drugs than hurt you."

A stiff smile came to her lips. "Aw, you do care." She looked away and a loud sniff filled the air.

"What's going on?" Michael called from the end of the van.

"A guy was trying to steal drugs. Had Ellen at knife-point," Chance answered.

Michael climbed in, went to Ellen and gathered her into his arms. She buried her face in his chest. For some reason Chance wished he was the one she had turned to. He left the van and spoke to Marco, who'd already tied the man up, but his thoughts were still with Ellen. The trespasser admitted that he was with the injured man Michael had been caring for. The injury had been a small self-inflicted wound and used as a diversion.

The rest of the staff had to know what had happened in detail before they returned to packing up. Chance gave the short version on what he'd done before Ellen told her side. He was all too aware of Michael's arm around her shoulders the entire time. Why shouldn't she seek reassurance and comfort from him?

Marco would see to it that the Honduran authorities picked up the man they had captured and looked for the other two. Little would be done to them because Honduras had larger drug problems than these petty thieves.

Half an hour later it was dark and the trucks were loaded and ready to leave.

"Ellen, come on up here," Michael called from the cab of the truck. "I think you're still a little shaken up."

"I'm okay back here." She climbed in the rear with Karen and Peter.

She was tough. Chance admired her for that. After those few minutes of emotion with Michael she'd joined in and helped store the supplies, acting as if nothing had happened.

* * *

That evening at dinner Chance watched as Michael stood and tapped his fork against a glass.

"We have a few awards to give out tonight. First, to the great Dr. Freeman, for his heroic use of a van door to apprehend a drug dealer." Michael grinned. "Well done, Chance." He placed a second plate of dessert near him.

Chance smiled and nodded. Why did Michael have to make a big deal of what happen?

"And last but not least, to Dr. Ellen Cox, who held herself together under pressure and didn't give up the key to the drug cabinet." Michael held up his drink glass. The others joined him. A soft clinking of glass touching glass sounded around the room. "For you a flower." He bowed as he presented her with a large orange Bird of Paradise.

Ellen smiled but it didn't quiet reach her eyes. Had she been and was she still more scared than she let on?

"Chance deserves all the accolades. I did nothing." Ellen looked directly at him with sincerity in her eyes. "Thanks for saving me."

Examining the terror coursing through him when he'd realized Ellen was being threatened was something he didn't want to look at too closely. The emotion had been too strong, raw. Still he couldn't deny the relief that had replaced the terror when he'd known she was okay.

Satisfaction he'd not felt in a long time filled him. His look held hers as he nodded. Why did he suddenly feel like standing and thumping his chest?

Ellen rolled to the left and minutes later to the right. She'd been trying to sleep for hours. The sound of rain with the steady dripping off the hut roof would normally lull her to sleep but not tonight. At least the adrenalin rush she'd experienced today should have had her in a deep sleep but it didn't seem to come.

She rubbed the back of her neck. The feel of the man's breath on her skin and the prick of the tip of the knife remained. Even after a hot shower and neck massage the ache between her shoulders blades remained. Would it ever go away? Could she forget that feeling of helplessness? Fear for the others?

It had been that same feeling she'd had when she'd been trapped in the car with her mother. They had been making a simple trip to buy Ellen a dress. It had been a pretty day but the traffic had been heavy. Her mother had sped up to go through a traffic light that had turned yellow. The next thing Ellen had known they'd been upside down and her mother's blood had been everywhere.

Her mother had said, "Your father always says I take too many chances." Then the life had left her.

Slinging the covers away, Ellen slid out and grabbed the thin blanket off the end of the bed, wrapping it around her shoulders. She headed out the front door. Maybe if she watched the rain for a few minutes she could sleep.

She walked to the porch rail. The shower had eased and a full moon was making an appearance every now and then behind the clouds. When it did the soft glow made the raindrops on the ferns surrounding the hut glisten. She stood there, absorbing the peace.

"Can't sleep?"

She yelped and spun toward Chance's hut. He climbed out of the hammock wearing nothing but tan cargo shorts that rode low on his hips. She couldn't help but stare. "Have you been there since I came out?"

"Yep."

"Why didn't you say something?" she snapped.

"I thought you needed a few moments to yourself. What happened today can be hard to process."

He wiped all the times he'd been less than warm away

with one compassionate comment. "Yeah, it got to me more than I wanted to admit at dinner."

He came down the steps and started toward her hut. "You wouldn't be human if it hadn't affected you. And you are very human."

She looked down at him. Her heart fluttered as she watched his half-naked body coming toward her. "What's that supposed to mean?"

He started up her steps. "That you're one of the most empathetic and naturally caring doctors I've ever worked with. You feel things more strongly than most. There's no way you wouldn't be upset about being held at knife-point."

"Wouldn't anyone be?" How did he know so much about her when they'd only known each other such a short time?

He came to stand an arm's length. "Sure they would, but I have a feeling you were not only worried about yourself but the rest of us. Or what would happen to the local boy if you gave up the drugs. Your heart is too tender for this type of work."

"I thought caring was what it took to work here." She continued to watch a small stream of water flow over a large leaf and to the ground.

"Yeah, but it also makes for a great victim."

Ellen turned to face him, propping a hip against the rail. She was no victim. When her mother had died she'd proved that. "You know, there was a moment there that I thought you might be trying to cheer me up. I should have known better."

"Look, you did good today. Held it together. I don't know if anyone could have done better. How was that?"

The corner of her mouth lifted. "Better. But it lacked a ring of sincerity. By the way, I really do appreciate you saving me."

"That's what I do, save people."

Was he embarrassed by the praise? "You make it sound like it's no big deal but to them it is. And to me it was."

He bowed. "Then you're welcome. Let's just hope I don't have to do it again."

This time she had the idea that his words were to cover up his awkwardness at being thought a hero. "It would suit me just fine for it not to happen again as well."

Chance moved toward the steps. "We have another early morning so you best get to bed."

"I'm sorry if I woke you."

He looked up at her from the walk. "Not a problem. The view was well worth it."

"Uh…"

"A woman in the moonlight dressed in a sexy see-through gown is always worth being woken up for. Get some sleep. You'll need it tomorrow."

Yeah, as if she was going to sleep after that statement.

Two days later Ellen scanned the clinic area. Since the incident with the vandals, she looked over her shoulder any time she was alone. Being held at knifepoint had rattled her more than she wanted to show. She had been paralyzed by fear. No way was she going to let on how much what had happened in the van stayed with her. If she showed weakness around Chance, he would see to it that she was sent home. She was determined to stay and continue her work. Ellen was surprised to find that she'd drifted off to sleep after their conversation on her porch. He'd managed to make her think of something else besides what had happened. She wouldn't have thought that was possible. Had his last remark been to get the incident off her mind or had he meant what he'd said?

She glanced at him working at the next exam table. He was great with the patients and got along with the others in the group. Was even known to laugh on occasion. It was a wonderful full sound. He didn't treat her differently in an obvious way but she sensed something…perhaps that he was weary of her for some reason. Her assignments were almost always with Michael. That suited her. At least she didn't have to deal with Chance's moods or with her uncontrollable thirst to understand him better.

Chance never sat beside her if there was a choice of another open chair at dinner. They were never alone even if they were going to their huts at the same time. Apparently for him to approach her porch had been completely out of character. It was as if she had the plague and he was highly susceptible. Sometimes she thought about just forcing the issue and asking him what his problem was, but why should it matter? She had come to Honduras to work, not to get caught up in the great Dr. Chance Freeman's life.

And she was working. Hard. It was invigorating. The days were long but satisfying. It was as if she had been liberated from a cage. She belonged here. Her father may not like it but she wouldn't be returning to New York to work ever again.

Minutes later Karen was called to assist Michael with a patient while Ellen was still doing a wound cleaning. When she finished Karen and Michael were still involved with the patient so she was left with no choice but to help Chance.

"Ellen, would you mind calling the next patient?"

She did as he asked. A highly deformed man entered the tent with the help of a woman who Ellen guessed was his mother. The man had elephantiasis. His arms and legs were enlarged, as were areas of his head and neck. She couldn't prevent her intake of breath. The only case she'd ever seen had been in a medical textbook.

"We mustn't make him feel unwelcome," Chance said

from close enough behind her that she felt the warmth of his body.

He spoke to the man in Spanish and he returned a lopsided smile that appeared sincere.

"Ricardo is one of my regular patients."

"Hello, Ricardo," Ellen said, giving him her most genuine smile. "Nice to meet you."

Ricardo gave her the same smile he'd given Chance.

"We're going to need to get some blood work today, Ricardo." Chance said, pulling on gloves.

The man nodded and spoke but it came out as gibberish.

Ellen went to get a blood sample kit. She returned and Chance said, "Ricardo, do you mind if Ellen draws your blood?"

Ricardo nodded his head in agreement. As she pressed to find a good vein Ricardo said, "Pretty."

"Yes, she is," Chance answered as he continued to examine Ricardo.

She smiled at Ricardo. "Thank you. You are very sweet."

Even with his distorted face she could see his discomfort. This man was a gentle giant who'd been given a bad deal in life by contracting elephantiasis.

Chance finished his examination and gave Ricardo a supply of antibiotics before he left. With him gone Chance asked, "You've never seen someone with a major case of elephantiasis, have you?"

"No. I had no idea. I'm sorry I reacted poorly."

"Don't worry about it. It's hard not to."

There was that compassion she rarely saw but which pulled her to him. "What can you really do for him?"

"For right now he's getting the antibiotic diethylcarbamazine but that only really deals with the symptoms. He has lymphatic filariasis. It's from worms introduced by mosquitoes. It's common in the tropics. Ricardo is just one of many. If you stay around long enough you will see more. Ricardo's case is getting bad enough he'll need surgery to keep walking."

"Where will he go to have that?"

"I had hoped we would have a standing hospital built by now but we're still working on the funding. Right now he'll have to go to the city or hope a visiting group of orthopedists is able to come here."

"That's sad." Her heart hurt for Ricardo and the others like him. These people needed more help.

Their next patient entered and ended their conversation but the needs in the small tropical country remained on Ellen's mind. Chance was working hard to do what he could but it wasn't enough. What would happen if he didn't get the funding required and the clinic closed?

The rest of the afternoon was one more patient after another. Once again a storm built and seemed primed to dump water over them. As much as Ellen enjoyed rain, every day was a little much. Thirty minutes after the last patient was seen the clinic was dismantled and she, Karen and Peter were running for the truck as the first fat drops of water fell.

"You guys will be drenched. We're going to have to double up in the cabs," Michael yelled over the sound of thunder and wind. "Ellen, you go in the van. Karen and Peter, we'll just have to make do in the truck cab."

The rain started coming down in sheets. Ellen didn't hesitate before running to climb into the van. Marco was already in the driver's spot. Her bottom had hardly hit the seat before she was being pushed across it by Chance. His body leaned heavily against hers as he slammed the door. He moved off her but she was still sandwiched between him and Marco. The gearshift on the floor forced her legs into Chance's space. She shifted to an upright position but remained in too close contact with him.

"Maybe I should just ride in the back of the truck," she murmured.

Chance looked out the window shield. "Not in this storm. Scoot over."

"To where? I'm practically sitting in Marco's lap now." She shifted away from him but it made little difference. Her right side was sealed to his left from shoulder to knee.

Marco put the truck into gear and it launched forward. They hadn't gone far when the truck hit a bump that almost brought her down in Chance's lap. She squirmed away from him. Gritting her teeth, she did her best not to touch him any more than necessary. Her mind as well as her body were hyperaware of even his breathing. She'd be sore in the morning from her muscles being tense in her effort to put space between them.

The storm continued to rage around them as they traveled over the muddy roads. Finally, they reached the poorly maintained paved road. She was exhausted and the cab was warm and steamy. With the steady swish-swish of the wipers the only sound in the cab, Ellen's chin soon bobbed toward her chest. Sometime during the ride her head came to rest against a firm cushion.

A hand on her arm shook her. "We're home."

Ellen jerked straight. She'd been leaning against Chance's shoulder. "I'm sorry. I didn't mean to fall asleep on you."

He ignored her, reached for the door handle and said a little stiffly, "Since it's so late we won't be eating in the dining room tonight. A supper tray will be brought to your hut."

A light rain fell as she climbed down from the van. "I'm glad. I don't think I have the energy to walk up to the main building."

Karen joined them and handed Ellen her backpack. "I'm headed for a hot shower and bed."

"Me too," Ellen agreed. "I'll walk with you. Good night," she said to the group in general.

"We have another early morning tomorrow. Be here ready to go at six a.m.," Chance called after them.

Karen mumbled, "Slave driver."

Ellen giggled. "And a few other things."

Foliage dripped around them and the moon shone above as they walked along the path toward their huts.

"Chance is something else, isn't he?" Karen said with admiration in her voice.

"He's something all right," Ellen mumbled.

"Very good looking, and super smart. I can see why the women that come down here are known to get crushes on him."

Ellen huffed. "Where did you get that bit of info?"

"Michael told me."

"Well, I won't be developing one, that's for sure." Ellen pushed a strand of escaped hair out of her face. Wasn't she already headed that way? She stood in front of Karen's hut.

She'd stopped at the top of her steps and looked at Ellen. "What is it with the two of you anyway?"

"He doesn't like me for some reason."

Karen gave her a searching look. "Aren't you over-reacting?"

"I don't think so. I'm too tired to worry about what Dr. Freeman thinks of me tonight. See you in the morning." Ellen continued along the path.

"Well, you're blind if you don't see how attractive he is," Karen called after her.

Ellen was well aware of how handsome Chance was but it wasn't enough to overlook his controlling and sometimes overprotective attitude where she was concerned.

The shower water couldn't get hot enough for her. Ellen stood in it until it started to cool. She loved this shower. It was almost like she was skinny dipping. With a towel wrapped around her, she entered the back door of the hut just as a light came on in Chance's. She watched as he pulled his safari shirt off over his head and let it drop to the floor. From her vantage point she was a voyeur but she couldn't stop herself from looking.

Chance was older than any other men she had been attracted to but he still had a nice body. He flipped his belt out of the clasp then looked up. It was as if they were standing inches apart and he was reading her every thought. Heat flashed over her. She released the blind but it hadn't fallen between them before she saw a sexy grin cross his lips.

CHAPTER THREE

CHANCE LAY BACK in the lounger located in a recess surrounded by plants near the pool. Only a person who looked carefully or passed him could see him, while he had an open view of most of the water. He needed some down time, just like the others. Thank goodness Friday was the transition day for guests so this afternoon there were few around. The resort would be full for the week by the next evening.

He'd worked his staff hard over the last week. They had moved to five different areas in five days, with each day starting at four a.m. The team not only needed a break but deserved one. Michael had volunteered to show the others around Trujillo. Karen and Peter had taken him up on the suggestion but for some reason Ellen had declined to join them. Chance had paperwork to see to and a conference call to make so he'd remained behind as well. He'd not seen Ellen since that morning and assumed she was resting in her hut.

In the short time since the three new staff members had arrived, their clinic team had turned into a cohesive group that worked well together. Ellen had assisted him some but mostly he'd stationed her with Michael or given her triage duty. She and Michael had become regular buddies. When there weren't patients to see, they had lunch together, laughing over something that had happened. It reminded him too much of Alissa and his ex-colleague Jim.

Even Marco and his crew gave Ellen special attention. She shared her sunshine with everyone but him. It wasn't that she wasn't civil, it was just that he didn't receive the same warmth. The times she had worked with him they had said little outside the need-to-know arena. He shouldn't have cared but he felt left out. When she'd first arrived he'd wanted it that way but now he wasn't so sure. The more he was around her the more he admired her. She wasn't the pampered princess he'd wanted to believe she was.

Ellen was an excellent doctor. When she was working triage she recorded what was wrong and had everyone in order of need so that no time was wasted between patients. Maybe it was time to let her start handling patients on her own. They could see three times more patients if he did.

After the excruciating return ride to the resort, when she'd fallen asleep against him, and later, when he'd caught her watching him undress, he'd renewed his vow to stay clear of her as much as possible. He'd be lying if he said he hadn't enjoyed the feel of a soft body against him. But wouldn't he have reacted the same to any female contact?

There wasn't much opportunity for a sex life around here but when he'd found companionship he'd been discreet about it. After his wife had left he'd been the favorite subject of discussion and he hadn't enjoyed it. He preferred his private life to remain just that—private. A few times in Honduras he'd met a woman of interest and when he'd return to the States he had a few ladies he regularly stayed in contact with, so he had hardly been celibate. Still, there was something about Ellen that made his hormones stand up and take notice whenever she was near, as if he had been a monk and left the order.

If the ride home hadn't been painful enough, the fact that she'd been watching him undress while wearing nothing but a towel had made him even more sexually aware. Every time they were alone it was like she was teasing him, daring him to come closer. He was confident this was something she did unconsciously yet it was still there, pulling him to her. As his body heated with need he imagined stepping across the short space between their huts and taking her in his arms. That would have shown her not to be poking the bear. Instead, she'd let the blind down, shutting him out.

He understood that feeling. In this case, he was glad she had. Even a short moment of pleasure would turn into a bad idea in the long run. Despite how she might act about work here, she wasn't the type to stay with him. No woman was. His life was in Honduras. She would never be satisfied with him or living here for the long run. He wasn't her prince charming.

Chance opened one eye to a slit at the soft pad of feet along the bricks around the pool. Ellen stood there in a blue bikini, preparing to dive. He shifted uncomfortably in the chair as his body reacted to all the beautiful skin on display. Her hair was down around her shoulders. The woman was going to be his undoing. He'd been played for a fool before and if he wasn't careful he would give Ellen the opportunity to do the same again.

With a perfect arch, she dove into the pool and surfaced. As she swam to one end and back, he was fascinated by each smooth movement she made. What he wouldn't do to be the water flowing around her. He had to get some control but that wasn't going to happen right now. On her next pass he stood. Hopefully his baggy swim trunks would disguise most of his body's reaction to her.

A yelp of surprise came from her when he stepped into her view.

"Hey." He watched as all that long blonde hair swirled around her on the surface of the water.

"Hi. I didn't see you sitting there."

He stepped closer. "I thought you would've gone to town with the others."

"I thought about it. But I hate to admit that after the pace we've kept this week I needed a little extra rest. I can be a tourist on our next day off."

"Do you like being a tourist?"

"I do. I love to see new places. See how others live." She held on to the edge of the pool.

Her position gave him a tantalizing view of her breasts scantly covered in triangles of dark blue that reminded him of a sky just before a storm. "So what do you think of Honduras?"

"I like it. The people are wonderful. Every day is exciting."

"Some days, too much so." Like the day she had almost been stabbed. It still sent fear though him when he thought about it.

Ellen pushed away and floated toward the other side of the pool. Chance took a seat on the edge, letting his feet dangle in the water.

"So why aren't you off doing something exciting on your day off? Surely you get away from work sometimes," she asked.

"Not as much as I would like." He enjoyed watching her tread water. She had managed to put as much space as possible between them. For that he was grateful. He was far to attracted to her. "When I get a couple of days I like to spend them scuba diving. Hiking in the jungle."

She moved closer. "I would love to learn to scuba dive. My father said no when I was a kid. Never took the time to learn after I started college. And hiking? After all the lectures you've given me about safety, you hike in the jungle?"

"I stay on the touristy trails. More than one person has gotten into trouble, venturing off too far."

"Michael offered to take me to see a waterfall one day." With a kick, she swam away from him again.

"I wouldn't get too attached to Michael if I were you." Chance didn't like how that sounded. Like a jealous middle-schooler. "Hey, I shouldn't have said that. It's none of my business what you two do after hours."

She headed for deeper water. "I'm pretty sure Michael flirts with every woman in his age group who comes down here. I don't take anything he says seriously."

That's what his wife had said when he'd questioned her about her relationship with Jim. Still, coming from Ellen he wanted to believe her.

"Anyway, I'm down here to work, not play around." She started toward the shallow end.

"But it's always nice to have a friend."

Could they be friends? He wasn't so sure. This attraction would also be vibrating between them.

"Well, I think I'll get a nap in before dinner. See you later." Ellen took the steps out of the pool, giving him a tantalizing view of her backside that included a sexy swing of her hips.

Chance slipped into the water and began making strong, sure laps until he was exhausted.

Ellen paused in the doorway of the restaurant. Maybe she'd just eat in the main dining area tonight. She'd given thought to having her meal brought to her hut but she wasn't going stay in such a beautiful place and hole up in her room.

She'd made it halfway to the private dining room when her name was called. She recognized that voice.

Chance sat at a table overlooking a bubbling water fixture among ferns. A candle flickered in the lantern on the table. "We have to eat out here tonight. Not enough of us to prepare the extra room for. You're welcome to join me but I'm almost done."

She looked around the area at all the empty tables. Hating to cause any of the staff more work, she still wasn't sure she wanted to eat a meal with Chance in such a romantic setting. Maybe she should order her food then make an excuse to carry it back to her hut. "Okay."

Chance half stood as she took her seat cross from him.

After feeling vulnerable at the pool in nothing but her swimsuit, she wasn't sure she could handle more time between the two of them. Every nerve in her body had been aware of Chance watching her leave the pool. It had been exciting and terrifying at the same time.

Apparently she was worrying for no reason. Chance ate and shuffled papers he had spread out on the table without paying any notice to her. She finally asked, "So what are all these?"

"Med invoice forms. I'm expecting a shipment any day." He didn't look at her.

"You do work all the time."

He glanced up. "Someone has to do the paperwork."

"Can't someone else do that?"

He made an exaggerated scan of the room. "You see someone else volunteering?"

"I'll be glad to. It wouldn't hurt you to accept help sometimes."

He put down the paper he had been reviewing. "Do you always say what you're thinking?"

"Not always." She certainly didn't where her father was concerned and kept some of her thoughts about him to herself.

A waiter showed up with her meal. They fell into silence as they both ate. For some reason she didn't even think to ask to take her meal to the room. "You know, I could help with those. I'm a pretty good organizer. Maybe I can set up a system that'll make it easier for you."

"Don't you get enough work during the day not to want more?"

She shrugged. "I want to help. That's what I'm here for."

He looked at her. "And why is that? Here in Honduras?"

"Because of you." She wanted that passion and conviction she'd heard in his voice in her life.

"That's right, you said. Where was the fund-raiser?"

"In New York about six months ago." She'd spent the next few months trying to convince her father that her life's calling was in Honduras. He'd spent the time fighting the idea.

"That long ago."

"Yeah, it took me awhile but I made it."

Chance looked at her instead of the papers. "Why not sooner?"

"Well, mostly because of my father."

Chance lifted his chin in question. The man had a way of getting people to talk to him. He was practicing that bedside manner she'd seen him use on his patients. It was powerful when turned on someone. She was that person now. The feeling that if he turned up the charm she couldn't resist him anything filled her. Caution was what she needed to use.

"I'm an only child with an overprotective father. Make that way overprotective."

"I guess if I had a beautiful daughter and she wanted to come down here to work I'd be concerned also."

He'd said she was beautiful. Other men had but for some reason she especially liked hearing it from Chance.

"I love my father but after my mother died he just couldn't stand the thought of losing me too. He seemed to think that making all the decisions in my life was the answer to keeping me safe."

"He wouldn't be pleased to know what happened the other day, would he?"

"No, he wouldn't, and I don't plan to tell him. It would only worry him. He already thinks I take too many risks."

"Risks?"

"Yeah, like going into medicine, working in an inner-city clinic, or like coming down here."

"Then I'd better see that you get home safe."

Anger shot though her. "That's not your job. I can take care of myself. I don't need someone else watching over me."

"Whoa." He held up a hand. "I stepped on a tender spot. Sorry." He went back to looking at his papers.

Taking a deep breath, she focused on her meal again. She watched the candle flicker and listened to the tinkle of water in the fountain then glanced at Chance. He was a handsome man. One of those who drew a woman's attention naturally. There was an aura about him that just made her want to know him better. But what she didn't need was someone caging her after she'd finally found her freedom.

Done with her meal, she asked, "Of all the places in the world, why did you decide to start a clinic in Honduras?"

Chance looked up. "I came here to do summer work with one of my professors while in med school."

"That was it. You decided to start the Traveling Clinic?"

"Yeah, something like that. I saw the hardship and wanted to work here."

Something about his tone made her think there was more to it than that. "So you decided to make it your life's work."

"It sort of evolved into it." He took a bite of the fruit they'd been served for dessert.

"How's that?"

Chance put his fork down. "You're full of questions."

"No more than you were."

"Okay, so I had high hopes that I could make life better for the Hondurans. Make a real difference. But that, like everything else, costs money. Each year that has been harder to come by."

"So when you made fun of me for trying to save the world you weren't any different your first time in Honduras."

A sheepish look came over his face. "Yeah, I know that stars-in-the-eyes look. I've had it and seen it hundreds of times. I've also seen people go home defeated by the amount of need here."

"Is that why you're so tough on me, because you don't want me to be discouraged?"

He crossed his arms on the table. "I just want you to understand what you're getting into. This isn't a fairy-tale world."

"What makes you think I need that?"

"Look at you. Your polished nails. You don't belong here. This isn't a place for you."

She leaned toward him. "Who gave you such a narrow view of women and their abilities?"

"That would be my ex-wife, who came down here and stayed a few months before she left me for my colleague."

By the tone of his voice he was still terribly bitter. She

couldn't keep the amazement in her voice from showing. "You were married?"

"Don't sound so surprised. Even I can make a mistake."

"Mistake? That's a sad view of marriage."

"But honest. Enough on that subject." Chance returned to the papers at his fingertips.

He had been hurt, deeply. Did he judge all women by his ex-wife's behavior? Even her? Maybe that's why he treated her so unfairly. A few minutes later, she pushed back from the table. "Thank you for the stimulating company but I think I'll call it an evening."

To her disbelief Chance gathered his work, stood and stuffed the forms in his back pocket. "I'll walk back with you."

She didn't question his motives; instead, she said thank you to the waiter and headed for the door. Chance caught up with her and they walked out of the main building.

She needed to apologize for spying on him but she couldn't bring herself to say anything. They continued walking.

At her hut Ellen said, "Uh, about the other night, the window and all. I'm sorry."

"Don't be. I was flattered."

She shifted from one foot to the other, not meeting his eyes. "Still, I shouldn't have been invading your privacy. It won't happen again."

"That's a shame. I found it flattering."

"Why am I not surprised?" Where she had been embarrassed now she was indigent. He was enjoying her discomfort.

"What man doesn't appreciate a lovely woman admiring him?"

"My, you have an ego."

He grinned. "I'm just teasing you."

"Since when do you tease?"

"Maybe I'm finding a new side to my life."

"Could another one be you getting over your issues with me?"

Suddenly the current of awareness between them went up three notches. The air almost sparked. He stepped into her personal space. "Sweetheart—" the word was more growl than endearment "—I don't think so. I have too many where you are concerned. The main one is wanting you."

Her heart quickened. She'd not anticipated that declaration. In fact, by the way he'd treated her she hadn't been sure he even liked her. Chance stepped closer. She refused to back away. His head lowered and an arm went around her waist. He drew her against him. His mouth found hers and she forgot to think. She hung on for dear life. It wasn't a simple meeting of lips. Too many emotions roiled in her and flowed between them. The kiss was a mixture of shock, amazement, taking, giving, and abrupt release.

Without a word Chance left her staring after him as he stalked off past his hut and up the path.

On weak legs Ellen slowly climbed the steps to her porch. What had brought that on?

For days he'd treated her as if she was an interloper in his world. Out of nowhere he'd kissed her like there was no tomorrow.

Then he'd abruptly let her go. Why? What had suddenly turned him against her? There had been something real between them and just as quickly he'd broken the connection as if it was something he wanted no part of. Her arms went around her waist and she squeezed. Being pushed away hurt.

She knew what she had been thinking. No one had kissed her like that in her life. The electric ripple had rolled through her, making her ultra-aware of her body and his. She'd come close to marrying other men who had never had that effect on her. What if she had never known those brief moments of passion with Chance?

How far would she have allowed Chance to go? By her reaction to his kiss, too far. She bit her lower lip. Even now her lips still tingled.

But could she afford to act on her feelings again? Coming to Honduras had been her way of finding her place in the world. A space she chose and to make hers. Not one that her father oversaw or controlled. Did she want to get involved in something that might hurt her chances of staying here?

It really wasn't an issue. Chance had walked way.

Chance hesitated at the bottom step to Ellen's hut. He had no choice but to knock on her door. Never having been an indecisive person, he couldn't understand why this time it was so difficult to do something so simple. Maybe because he was afraid she'd chew him out for the abrupt way he'd grabbed her, kissed her and walked off. He deserved her disdain even if he had done the right thing. Now he had a larger issue. A shipment of drugs was coming in and he needed to meet the plane. She'd offered to help with the paperwork and this was one of the times he needed her.

Needed her. Unfortunately, that seemed to be happening on a number of levels.

He prided himself on facing problems head on but the thought of approaching Ellen so soon after their kiss had him feeling uneasy. The kiss they'd shared had rattled his nerves and his convictions. He wanted more than a kiss and that shook him to the core. She shouldn't interest him, shouldn't affect him in any way, but she did, far too much. He'd spent the night vacillating between berating himself and wanting to crawl into Ellen's bed. The latter he wasn't going to do under any circumstances. He had to stop whatever was happening before it got out of hand.

He wouldn't kiss her again.

For him, controlling his emotions had been a lifetime thing. He done it when his mother had left, when his father had sent him to boarding school, separating him and his sister, and yet again when the headmaster had stated frankly he would never amount to anything. He would do so again where Ellen was concerned. It was necessary if he didn't want to lose his sanity, or, worse, hurt her.

She was a good doctor and he was as well. They were in Honduras to help people and that was what they would do. Their relationship would remain professional. He wasn't some teen whose body ruled his brain or some lovestruck young man who went after the first beautiful woman he'd seen in a while. As a mature man he could handle any fascination he might feel for her, especially a woman he wasn't sure he liked.

Chance gave the door a sharp, solid tap. There was no response. His knuckles rapped against the wood once more.

"Coming." The word had a groggy sound.

Ellen opened the slatted door and stood on the other side of the screen door.

"Did I oversleep?" Panic filled her voice.

Her mass of hair fell in disarray around her face. The temptation to open the door, take her in his arms and walk her backwards to the bed almost got the better of his control. How much was a man supposed to take? Chance sucked in a breath.

"No. Were you serious about helping with the paperwork?" He sounded gruff and formal even to his own ears.

She blinked twice. "Yes."

"Then I need you to come with me. We have a shipment.

I want to show you how to handle it and what's involved."
He was already making his way down the steps again.

"Okay. Give me ten minutes."

"I'll get us something to eat and meet you at the truck."
He didn't wait for her to answer before heading along
the path.

As good as her word, which he was coming to learn
was ingrained in Ellen's makeup, she showed up at the
Jeep dressed and ready to go right on time. He'd never
known a woman as attractive as she who could be dressed
on such short notice. His ex-wife would have certainly
balked at his request, expecting at least an hour to prepare herself to go out in public, even in the wee hours of
the morning.

Ellen climbed into the seat beside him and he handed
her a cup of juice and a banana. "Breakfast of champions."

"Or the crazy," she mumbled.

Chance grinned. He found she had that effect on him
more often than most. There was never a dull moment
around Ellen. He was learning to like it. Putting the Jeep
in gear, he headed toward the road that would take them
to the nearby airstrip.

Ellen yawned. "Why so early? It's three a.m."

"This is when a plane was available to bring supplies
in. We use volunteers and have to work around their
schedule. This plane was making another delivery and
just added us as an extra stop."

"Oh. You couldn't have told me about this last night?
I would have been ready."

"I didn't know for sure and I had other things on my
mind." Like kissing you, holding you, taking you to bed.

A soft sound of realization came from her side of the
cabin.

"Uh, Ellen, about that kiss. Look, I'm sorry, I shouldn't
have done that. You didn't come down here to have an af-

fair and I certainly don't make it a habit of taking advantage of young women. It won't happen again." Out of the corner of his eye he saw her shift towards him in the seat.

"For starters, I'm old enough to take care of myself and I make my own choices about who I kiss, not you."

"But I took advantage of the situation..."

He felt her glare. "Chance, just shut up and drive."

Half an hour later they had reached the airfield. Marco and a couple of the others were helping set out lanterns along a dirt runway.

"This looks a little illegal to me," Ellen said as they waited on the plane circling the field.

"It would be by American standards but by Honduran ones it's the only way to get the drugs safely into our hands." Chance pointed toward a car sitting near the tree line. "That's one of the officials. We'll give him the papers, a little cash and he'll sign off on them."

"So it is illegal?"

"No, we just have to get our shipments in a less orthodox method so that we don't draw the drug traffickers' attention. This way we're not robbed on the road. Marco, Ricardo and Perez will ride as an armed escort back to the resort just to be sure."

"Is this how it's handled every time?" Ellen sounded excited by the whole idea.

"Pretty much, but we change up meeting points and times. Nothing's the same twice."

"Interesting. I kind of like this cloak-and-dagger stuff."

Chance grinned. He could see her as a femme fatale. "Rest assured, it's necessary and not something to take lightly."

The plane's wheels touched the runway, throwing up dust.

"Do you ever see the humor in something or do you always take everything seriously?"

"When it comes to my work it's serious."

And unfortunately where you are concerned it is serious as well.

Chance stepped on the gas and raced after the plane. They needed to have it unload and gone before anyone took notice. He pulled to a stop beside the plane. Thrusting some papers into Ellen's hand, he said, "As I call out the meds, you mark them off the list."

"Got it."

By the time he had the first box in his hands and was placing it in the trunk, Ellen was standing at the hood with a penlight in her mouth and the papers spread across it.

"Do you have a pen?"

"No."

She dug through her bag a second. "Never mind. I've got something."

"Amoxicillin."

"Okay," she called.

"Penicillin."

There was a pause. "Got it."

The government representative stood beside her as Chance named the medicine labeled on each of the boxes. The man didn't ask to see inside any of them. When it came time for him to sign the government form, Chance slipped him some bills and he went away smiling. The price of doing business. The process went on for another fifteen minutes.

Chance looked at Marco and his crew. "Okay, guys, are you ready to go?"

"*Sí.* We behind you."

Chance climbed into the Jeep. Ellen was already there, holding a paper by the corner as she flapped it. "What're you doing?"

"Making sure it's dry."

The paper must have sucked up moisture from the

night air. Chance breathed a sigh of relief that they were loaded and headed back to the resort. He was always on edge when waiting in the open. Drug traffickers were everywhere and as far as he and they were concerned his cargo was gold. The antibiotics were not the most valuable of drugs for resale but they certainly were important to the work of the clinic.

He glanced at Ellen. She'd gathered the forms firmly in her hands. He started the Jeep and they were soon turning into the resort entrance and driving round to the staff parking lot. Chance pulled into a slot next to the van. He waved at Marco as he turned in behind them then back out again on his way home.

"Marco isn't staying?"

"No, we're safe here. Now we need to get these counted and stored." Chance opened the back end of the van.

"How can I help?"

How like Ellen not to complain and join in. "As I bring you the boxes, open them, count the contents and store them in the lockbox."

"Will do."

Over the next half hour they worked together, getting the medicine into place. Ellen did everything he asked. With all the boxes in the van, he joined her inside it as well. Being in the tight area with her made him even more aware of his desire. Working shoulder to shoulder, with hands brushing on occasion, he questioned his judgment at having Ellen help him over asking Karen.

He'd chosen Ellen because she had offered and seemed good at this type of work. The other part of his reasoning had been to see how she reacted to the clandestine operation that was sometimes necessary. He was pleased, she'd come through like a champ.

With the medicine stored, Chance climbed out of the van and offered his hand to Ellen. She hesitated a second before she placed hers in his then jumped the short distance to the ground.

To his disappointment she let go of his hand. "Bedtime."

She yawned. "Past it."

"Tomorrow's clinic is in a village not far away. You and I will sleep in. The others will go ahead and we'll catch up with them before midmorning."

She pulled her bag out of the Jeep. "I can go earlier if I'm needed."

"No, you need your rest."

"But—"

What was the problem? The idea that she'd have to ride out with him? Or she wanted to spend time with Michael? "No buts. Be here at nine ready to go."

"Okay, but before I go I need to ask you a question." It had been worrying her all night. Ellen had to get some kind of answer for his behavior in front of her hut.

He stopped and turned. She moved toward him. Looking him straight in the eyes, she asked, "Why did you kiss me?"

A stillness came over Chance then he wiped his hand over his face. "Let's not get into it again. I've already apologized. It won't happen again."

"You didn't answer my question." Ellen refused to back down until he gave a reason. She said softly, "Why?"

"What do you want me to say? Because I wanted to more than anything in the world."

Did he mean that? Joy swelled in her chest. She stepped closer. "If that's the truth, why not?"

"Come on, Ellen, this isn't a good idea."

"Probably not. But I still want to know." She continued to study his face in the dim light.

"Look, you deserve more than I can or am willing to give."

"I don't remember asking for anything. And if I was, you don't get to decide that for me. My father has done that all my life and I don't need you taking his place. I choose what I want." Since when did he think she wasn't capable of making her own decisions?

"The most that can be between us is an affair. You don't want that. Go to bed, Ellen. Forget about what happened."

"Just for the record, I asked about a kiss, you are the one that brought up an affair. Good night, Chance."

That would give him something to think about. She took the path leading to their huts.

After a few hours of sleep, which were not refreshing by any standard, Ellen was sitting in the truck, waiting for Chance. She'd decided after their discussion that she would do her job, be as much help as she could be to the clinic, and stay out of Chance's way. He'd made it clear where he stood regarding her and she would respect that. That was just as well for her, she didn't need to get involved with someone who thought they knew all the answers where her life was concerned.

Chance walked up looking as if he hadn't fared any better since they'd parted than she had. His hat was crammed on his head and his aviator sunglasses were in place.

"Good morning," she offered.

Chance climbed into the driver's seat. "Mornin'."

"It came around pretty quickly."

A grin covered his lips. The one she didn't see often. "Nights like last night remind me I'm not as young as I used to be."

"I can understand that," Ellen mumbled as he started the Jeep and pulled out of the lot.

She looked at Chance's large, capable hands on the steering wheel and then moved her eyes up to his face to settle on his mouth. She like his full lips that remained far too serious far too often. As he slowed, her attention went to his strong thigh muscles flexing and contracting as he pressed the gas pedal after shifting gears.

He intrigued her, made her want to know more about him, figure out what made him react to her as he did. It wasn't just his kisses, his air of authority but his devotion to the people he was trying to help that fascinated her. Yet the hurt from the night before wasn't easy to let go of. There was still an ache behind her heart. No one liked being rejected, especially when they were told it was for their own good.

Ellen peeled an orange that she had taken from the bowl in her hut. Breakfast had been delivered without her request. It was her guess that Chance had seen to it. "Want some?"

"No, thank you."

"You sure?" She offered a couple of slices, holding them out. "I bet you didn't eat much for breakfast."

After shifting gear again, he reached out and took the slices from her.

A shiver of warmth went through her. All it took was one innocent touch and her heart rate jumped. If she was going to keep her promise to herself, she would have to get a handle on her reaction to Chance.

Ellen pulled a slice off the orange and popped it into her mouth, making an effort not to let it show how rattled she was. What she needed to do was focus on something else. "Tell me what you need done to get the paperwork in order."

"I have to see that everything is turned in on time and

in order to the foundation as well as to the government representative. I need help doing what we did last night and an inventory of supplies done regularly. I also need shipments set up. Have papers in order for customs."

For the next few minutes Chance continued to list different areas where he needed assistance.

"Where's the paperwork right now?" Ellen threw the orange peel out of the window.

"Most of it is on a table in my hut."

He was a control freak? Did he think he could do everything? "Have you been seeing to it since the clinic opened?"

"Pretty much, but lately it has been more difficult. The foundation is now required to submit items it didn't have to in the past. I have to admit I hate doing it as well."

"But you didn't plan to ask for help, did you?"

He glanced at her. "I let you help last night, didn't I?"

Chance had, but she had a feeling that was a rarity. She suspected she should feel honored.

By the time she and Chance arrived at the clinic area there was a line of people waiting.

"I should have come on with the others," Ellen said as she hopped out of the car. "So many waiting."

"It doesn't do them any good if you're so tired that you don't know what you're doing. They'll be seen. We won't leave until we do." Chance grabbed his to-go bag off the backseat.

He sounded like he knew from experience what bone tired meant. As if he'd been there before.

"I just hate the never-ending need here."

A weary look came over Chance's face. "I know what you mean. I often wonder if we'll ever make headway."

The statement was like a thump to her chest. She would've never thought she'd hear that discouraged tone from Chance. The great man who had stood at the podium and proudly shared the work being done in Honduras on behalf of the people. The work the clinic was doing. His voice made him seem demoralized. As if he could give up the effort. Didn't he see that just being here, his caring was making a real difference in these people's lives? Marco and his crew were better off just by the pay.

She walked beside him. "But it's worth it. We do make a difference. I see it in every place we go."

"Yeah, but it doesn't appear any different when we return. These people need local permanent clinics."

Was he just tired? She'd never heard him talk like this. "Then why do you keep on doing it?"

"Because no one else is. Where would these people go for help if the clinic wasn't here? Where would I go?"

A cloud of sadness settled around her. Why did he think he had no other place to go? What had happened to him? Where was his family?

Ellen followed Chance into the tent where the clinic was already in full swing. He took his spot at a table where Karen was prepping a patient for an exam. Peter was doing triage. Ellen joined Michael and went to work.

In the middle of the afternoon a mother brought in a baby who had a cleft palate. He was thin but had bright eyes. Not only his looks suffered from his mouth deformity but his ability to eat had as well. Ellen's heart went out to the child like it had to no other. The mother also had a three-year-old with her.

Michael lifted the older child onto the table. As he did the mother watched intently. Michael examined the boy and then said to the mother, "You'll need to clean this area."

The baby in her arms began to squirm.

"May I hold him?" Ellen asked.

The mother looked unsure but she handed the boy to Ellen.

She looked into the baby's face. With the right funding and the right people, how many children with cleft palates could be given a better life? Maybe she could get some support from her father and his contacts. Her fear was that in return his demand would be that she return to New York.

Michael said to her, "Chance will see the baby. He handles all the cleft palates."

Chance looked up when Michael called his name.

"Can you see this little boy now or do you want them to wait?" Michael asked.

"I'll be ready for him in a second."

He looked at Ellen, who was speaking baby talk to the child. She was absorbed in the child's happy but distorted sounds. Motherhood would suit her. She would make a good wife to someone. The idea left a sour taste in his mouth.

His voice was gruff when he said, "Ellen, bring him here and let me have a look."

She did as he asked.

"Hold him while I check him out." Chance pulled his stethoscope from around his neck and put the earpieces in place. He leaned close, placing the disk on the child's chest. The soft smell filled his nostrils. *Ellen*. Would her scent always remind him of flowers? She'd stopped wearing perfume after he'd explained it wasn't a good idea but still he would know her aroma anywhere.

Chance glanced up to find her watching him. They were so close he could see the black flecks in her blue eyes. He had to count the baby's heartbeats twice. Returning his attention to the child's chest didn't help matters. One of Ellen's breasts, covered in a tight T-shirt, was only inches from his hand. He dreamed of touching. Just once...

He closed his eyes and opened them again. Only by focusing on a tree outside the tent door was he able to record the child's respirations accurately the first time. The fascination with Ellen had to stop. Someone was going to notice. Worse, he was going to act on his desires.

The boy baby looked well cared for but thin. He would need surgery to continue to grow, for his teeth to form correctly and for him not to develop ear problems. Chance had just finished his examination when the mother, along with the older child, joined him and Ellen.

"Please continue to hold the boy," he said to Ellen. She smiled and nodded, appearing glad to do so. "I need to take some pictures." He then spoke to the mother, telling her he could help the child but that he would need surgery. That he wanted to take some pictures of the boy's mouth for the doctors.

The mother gave her agreement but she continued to look concerned.

"Ellen, I need you to hold him in front of you so I can get some pictures from different angles. Just stand where you are and try to keep him happy."

"That's not a problem. He's precious."

Chance hurried to the van and brought back the high-resolution camera then began taking pictures. The boy remained happily in Ellen's arms.

He wasn't surprised people were content around her. If it wasn't for the fact he was fighting his attraction to her all the time, he'd feel the same way around her.

Minutes later Chance had all the pictures he needed. "Ellen, get Marco to help you get all the information you can about names and where she lives so that we can contact her when the team comes down here. Marco knows what to do."

"Okay." She placed a kiss on the child's cheek and handed the boy back to his mother.

Despite the pretty picture, Chance was aware of the price of becoming too emotionally involved. Ellen would get hurt if she rushed in and opened her heart too freely.

He made sure that didn't happen to him.

Fifteen minutes later Ellen returned. He was between patients. "We got all the information you requested," she said.

"Good. The plastic surgery team should be here the week after next. We'll put the boy on the list. They'll have a full week of surgery."

"He's a cute little thing." She looked out the clinic door wistfully. "It's a shame he has to go through surgery."

"I could tell you liked him."

"How can you not?"

"Be careful, Ellen. Your bleeding heart is showing. Don't get too attached. You'll get hurt."

"You keep telling me that." She gave him a direct look. "Yeah, maybe. But if you never get attached you might miss out on something wonderful."

Pete asked her for some help and she left him. Chance had the idea that her remark had more to do with what was happening between them than dealing with their patients. He had closed himself off. Had meant to. How many times could he get kicked in the teeth and still survive? It had already happened twice. If he became involved with Ellen it would occur again. He was confident her kick would be the hardest of them all. He wouldn't give her up easily, but give her up he would.

CHAPTER FOUR

THE STAFF ATE supper together that night. Afterwards Ellen and Karen took a walk around the resort before heading for their huts. When Karen had said good-night and left, Ellen glanced at Chance's place. A light was on inside. She shrugged. Tonight would be as good a time as any to tackle those reports he was concerned about. Maybe he had time now to show her what needed doing.

A roll of thunder from the west arrived just as a soft rain began to fall. Ellen climbed the steps of Chance's hut. The main door was open. She knocked, at the same time looking through the screen.

"You looking for me?" The low rumble came from the hammock hanging near the edge of the porch.

Startled, she turned. "Are you spying on me again?"

"Hey, you're the one on my porch, looking into my hut."

The hammock swung slowly as he spoke. She stepped toward him, close enough to look down at him. Chance was stretched out with his hands behind his head and his legs crossed, wearing a T-shirt and cargo shorts. He appeared more relaxed than she'd ever seen him. Chance carried a heavy burden with all he did to make the clinic function. He deserved his down time.

"I came over to see if you wanted me to look at that

paperwork but I can see you're taking some time for your-self. We can do it tomorrow."

A streak of lightning flashed in the darkening sky seconds before thunder hit. Ellen yelped, jumped, and grabbed the rope supporting the end of the hammock where Chance's head lay. It swung. She tipped forward and down on top of him.

Strong arms circled her waist. "There's nothing to be afraid of."

With her palms she pushed against his chest. "I'm sorry. I didn't mean to fall on you."

Lightning flashed again. She shuddered.

"Don't worry, I have you."

There was security in those words. She looked into his eyes and found compassion there.

"It'll pass soon."

She relaxed into him. Found sanctuary. "Thanks. I've not been too fond of lightning since I was a child."

Chance continued to hold her but his body remained tense as if he was trying not to get too close, even though they were touching from shoulder to toes.

The lightning eased. She looked at him. "I think I'm good now. If you'll give me a little push, I can get off you."

Instead of doing as she requested, his lips found hers and her world exploded with pleasure. The hammock drifted to the side as he brought her up alongside him. She entwined her legs with his. He wore shorts and her bare legs brushed against his rougher ones. She stifled a moan.

Chance's hand slid down to cup her butt then squeezed it, lifting her against him. The knit tank top sundress she wore rode up her legs. He ran a hand along the back of a thigh, setting her skin tingling. She flexed into him. The evidence of his desire stood long and ridged be-tween them.

Ellen didn't question why Chance was kissing her after he'd made it clear earlier he didn't want her. She didn't care. He wanted her now. That was what mattered.

Chance's tongue demanded entrance and she gladly offered it. Her center throbbed. She was crazy for this man, had been since she'd heard him speak so passionately about the people he cared about. Even then she'd been half in love with him.

Vaguely aware of the rain falling around them as if curtaining them from the outside world, her hands shook as they pushed upward over his T-shirt and circled his neck, letting her fingers curl into his hair. His scalp was warm.

Chance's mouth left hers to nuzzle behind her ear. His fingers found her leg and the edge of her panties. Tracing the elastic, he teased her. His other hand splayed across her back, holding her close.

Ellen rolled her head to the side, giving Chance better access to her neck. He whispered, "Sweet, sweet El."

She slipped a hand under the hem of his shirt and found warm skin waiting there. His muscles rippled as her fingers brushed over them on her way around his waist to his back. It was heaven to touch Chance, to have him near.

His lips traveled over the line of her jaw and back to her mouth. He placed small hungry kisses on her mouth before he captured her lips completely in a hot kiss, full of need and question.

Ellen squeezed his neck and gripped his back, squirming against him.

"Woman, you're killing me."

"Good." Her lips found his and took command.

Abruptly Chance rolled forward, causing her to slide behind him, her face buried between his shoulder blades. The thump of steps on the boards of the porch stopped her complaint.

"Chance, I need to see you about your plans for the surgery team." At Michael's words Ellen went stone still.

"I'll meet you up by the reception area," Chance said.

"It'll just take a minute." Michael said.

Ellen grinned against Chance's back and brushed a fingertip over his waist. His hand captured hers and squeezed, holding it in place. Her body shook with a giggle.

Chance said tightly, "I'll see you up front."

There was silence for a second, then an "Oh…" from Michael. He added, with humor wrapping the word, "Gotcha."

As the sound of his footsteps disappeared, Ellen kissed the back of Chance's neck and ran her hands around his waist beneath his shirt. She snickered. "We almost got caught."

Chance's swung his feet to the floor and stood. He turned and offered her a hand. "I think you should go."

Really! She could kick Michael for showing up. Finally Chance was letting her in, showing his true feelings, and Michael barged in. Maybe she had been stepping over an edge that would end up hurting her but it would have been a wonderful trip down. Chance's touch sent her body into awareness overdrive.

As soon as Michael had left, Chance had turned cold. What was he afraid of? She wouldn't let him walk away as if nothing had happened. This time she wasn't going to stand for it.

Putting her hand in his, she let Chance pull her to a standing position. As soon as she had, he let her go and stepped back. She glared at him as she straightened her dress, then stepped close enough that her chest came into contact with his. His eyes widened but he didn't move. How much humiliation could she take?

"Dr. Freeman, I don't know what you're playing at but I'm tired of it. We're both adults. I'm old enough to know what I want and to be responsible for my decisions. I've made it clear I want you. I know you want me too. You made that obvious minutes ago. So give it a rest. It's not me you are protecting, it's yourself."

He said nothing but his jaw muscle jumped. She'd made her point. Shaking all over, she said, "I'll be going now."

Had he been gut punched? Chance stood there looking at the spot where Ellen had stood. He hadn't planned on what had happened. The second she'd fallen into his arms he'd been unable to let her go. If Michael hadn't walked up Chance had no doubt where it would have ended. His bed. Every fiber in his being wished it had.

Ellen was angry. She should be. He deserved every word she'd said. She felt used. What had he been thinking? That's just it, he didn't think around her. He'd wanted her to stay away. After tonight it looked like she would without him saying it again. Why didn't that make him feel better?

She been right about him protecting himself. He was afraid of her. Ellen had the capability of taking his heart and crushing it.

Inhaling a few deep breaths, he headed to the lobby area to meet Michael.

He was sprawled in a chair, flipping through a magazine as if he wasn't really interested in the material. When Chance approached, he sprang out of the chair with a wide grin on his face. "Sorry, man, I didn't mean to break something up. I had no idea."

Chance didn't want to talk about what had happened

between him and Ellen. His nerves were too raw. The need still too intense. "What do you need to know?"

"Oh, yeah, yeah. You're in a hurry to get back to Ellen."

Michael had seen her. Chance had tried his best to protect her. What was or wasn't between them, he wanted it to remain theirs alone.

Michael was saying, "I think it's great and about time. Ellen's crazy about you. I've tried to get something going but she'll have none of it. But you, she can't seem to keep her eyes off. Even when we're working she knows where you are all the time."

She did? Chance hadn't been aware. Maybe he hadn't wanted to. Regardless, he didn't want to discuss Ellen with Michael. "What did you need from me?"

Michael looked at him a second then said, "I need the list of patients and their diagnoses to fax to the surgery team ASAP."

"I need to double-check the info. Can I get them to you first thing in the morning?"

Michael grinned. "I'm sure that'll be soon enough."

"Good. See you then." Chance started back toward his hut.

A few minutes later he shuffled through the papers on his desk, the same ones that Ellen had come over to work on before he had distracted her. He looked at the drug list from a few nights before. Beside each drug there was a pink dot. What the hell?

That damn fingernail polish. The same that had covered her nails as she'd raked them over his skin just a few minutes earlier. And the ones he wished were still pulling him close.

He had to figure out a way around this obsession with Ellen. All he need to do was endure a few more weeks and she would be gone. The bigger question would be how would he survive after that?

* * *

Despite Ellen's anger with Chance, she was still basking in the glow of his kisses days later. She didn't like it but couldn't seem to do anything about it.

What would have happened if Michael hadn't interrupted them? Would Chance have forgotten all the opposition he'd put up against her and taken her to bed? Would she have let him? Could she have resisted?

Even now she wished she could be alone with him again. But she had no intention of allowing that. She wanted someone who trusted her to make her own decisions.

She looked at him sitting at the head of the table as if he were the patriarch of a family. Forking another piece of the succulent fruit off her dinner plate, she scanned the table. The staff was sitting down together for the first time in over a week. She relished it when they ate in their dining area, almost like they were a family. It had been just her father and her for so long that she enjoyed a meal with the large, boisterous group.

Chance tapped his fork against his glass. "Okay, listen up. Here's the plan for the next couple of days."

Everyone quieted.

"We'll be going to two outlying villages that are farther away from here than we normally go. Because of this, we'll have more armed guards than usual. Security will be extra-tight. We'll be in drug-trafficker country. They shouldn't bother us unless we give them a reason. And we'll be making every effort not to do that."

Ellen's newfound freedom shook a little. They were going to spend the night in the jungle? This was more than she'd expected when she'd decided to come to Honduras. She looked at Chance again. Everything was more than she'd expected.

"Is there a problem, Ellen?"

"No, sir."

His eyes narrowed at the use of *sir*. "You're welcome to stay here if you're not comfortable." His blue gaze bored into her. Daring her.

Was he trying get her to stay here? "No. I'm good. I wouldn't miss it."

His look moved to Peter and then Karen. They both nodded.

"Good. There has been some trouble with the local traders and we need to be very careful about every move we make. Don't ask any questions of the patients that aren't medical." He looked at her. "Don't leave the clinic area unescorted for any reason. My priority is everyone's safety. Take no chances. Pack for a two-night stay. Enjoy the comforts of home tonight because we'll be sleeping in the trucks or on the ground for the next couple of nights. Any questions?"

Ellen listened as the others talked and made comments about the plans. She couldn't decide if she was excited or terrified. Either way, this was the type of work she'd come to Honduras to do and she would do it without complaint.

"Pack light but be sure to have your long pants and long-sleeved shirts, hat and boots. Don't forget the bug spray and sunscreen." He looked at her. "This won't be a picnic. So be prepared."

He acted as if she had been complaining. Not once, to her knowledge, had she not risen to expectations. If she hadn't been sure she could do it she hadn't let on and had forged ahead. She was tired of trying to prove herself to him.

The next day consisted of a long drive into the interior of the country. Ellen had been told by Michael that the people they would be seeing had only seen a doctor a few times. She was looking forward to helping them.

She'd kept her distance from Chance whenever she

could. Disgusted with him for not facing the fact that he cared for her, she was also furious at herself for letting it matter. She was slowly accepting he was right. If they had a relationship and it went bad, she didn't think she could continue to work here. She would have to look elsewhere for a clinic. But would she like the country and the people as much as she loved this one? It would be better if they just remained professionals. But could she face Chance every day without her feelings showing?

They arrived at the village where they were to work by midafternoon. Before they had finished setting up people were waiting. Again, Ellen worked primarily with Michael, only occasionally swapping to help Chance. At those times they were almost too formal in their interactions. A couple of times the others gave them strange looks or knowing smiles. Would it be worse if they were together?

As the day ended, Marco and his men set up a food table. There were double the number of helpers, with two of them stationed on the perimeter of the area with rifles. Folding chairs were placed at the table so that everyone could sit in comfort to eat.

Growing up in New York City, Ellen hadn't had a chance to do any real camping. She'd attended summer camp but there had been beds with mattresses and running water. This was going to be rough camping and she was rather looking forward to the new adventure after the initial shock. The most interesting aspect so far was the tent structure with covered sides that had been set up as a bathroom area.

While they were eating Chance announced, "Ladies, you may have first turn in the bathroom. You'll find your sleeping bags in the back of the truck. Don't forget to pull the mosquito netting over you when you go to sleep.

Marco's men will be keeping watch tonight. Don't get up and wander around. Get some sleep. We'll start early tomorrow."

Ellen and Karen headed straight to the bathing area after dinner. They were allowed nothing more than a sponge bath but that was better than nothing. They changed into clean work clothes, which they would sleep in. Ellen left her bra off for ease of sleeping and planned to slip it on before anyone noticed in the morning. When she and Karen stepped out of the tent the men were already lined up, waiting to get in. Ellen pulled her towel up against her chest to cover the fact she was braless.

Chance was at the end of the line but she didn't met his gaze as she passed him.

There was a lantern burning in the truck and her and Karen's sleeping bags were already rolled out on the benches across from each other, their nets hanging from the side rails of the truck.

"I've always loved camping out," Karen said as she slipped into her bag.

"This is a first for me."

"Really? And no complaints. I like that about you. Always a good sport."

"Thanks. I wish others thought that." Ellen helped Karen adjust her net around her.

Karen lay back. "You really have a thing for Chance."

"I've sure tried not to." Ellen opened her bag.

"I've worked with many doctors but I've never seen one more dedicated than Chance. Sometimes people can't see past their job."

"I think most of it has to do with him thinking he needs to protect me."

Karen harrumphed then murmured, "It's more like the fact he has the hots for you that's bothering him."

He might but Chance had made it clear he wasn't going to act on them.

Ellen settled into her bag, turned the lantern down and pulled the net around her. Lying back, she looked up at the stars. This was an amazing country. Even with the poverty, need and sometimes danger she'd be happy to live here forever.

Sometime during the night Ellen woke, needing to go to the restroom. After debating having to get out of the sleeping bag, climb down out of the truck and walk across the camping area to the bathroom tent, she decided she had no choice. Using her penlight and moving as quietly as possible, she made her way there.

She was returning to the truck when a figure loomed near her. A hand touched her arm. She jerked away.

"Shush. You'll wake the whole camp." Chance stood close enough that she could feel his breath against her cheek. "What're you doing out here, wandering around? I've told you it isn't safe."

Ellen clenched her teeth. "I had to go to the restroom. Why should it matter to you anyway? You've made it clear you don't care about me."

Chance's fingers wrapped around her forearm and he pulled her behind the clinic tent, putting it between them and where the rest of the group slept. His arms crushed her against him and he growled, "You make me crazy. And the problem isn't that I don't want you but that I do." His mouth found hers.

Despite everything her brain told her about him hurting her again, her body told her to take what she could. She dropped her light and her hands clutched his waist. His tongue caressed the interior of her mouth and she join in the sweet battle. One of Chance's hands slipped under her shirt and slid over her ribs to cup her breast.

He groaned.

A flash of awareness went through her. Her flesh tingled. Reveled in Chance's touch. He took her nipple between two fingers and gently tugged.

Her womb contracted.

"Sweetheart," he murmured against her lips. He pushed the shirt higher. The moist night air touched her skin seconds before Chance leaned her over his arm. She held on as his wet, warm mouth covered her nipple and sucked. His tongue circled and teased her. Blood flowed hot and heavy to her center, feeding the throbbing there.

She moaned. Chance stood her up and his mouth covered hers. His hands went to her hips and brought them against his. With a hand behind his neck, she held his lips to hers.

"Mr. Chance, I heard a noise." Marco stood nearby.

Chance continued to hold her close as he said over his shoulder, "Everything is fine. Miss Ellen got lost. I'll see her back."

"*Si.*" By the tone of Marco's answer he saw through that lie.

With Marco gone, Chance tugged Ellen's shirt back into place. "Let's get you back to bed. We'll talk about this later."

Ellen's heart flew. At least this time he wasn't walking away mad, apologizing or denying that there was something between them.

He picked up her penlight then took her elbow, guiding her around the tent toward the truck. There he gave her a quick kiss and brushed her already sensitive breast with the knuckle of his index finger before he handed her the light and walked off into the darkness.

On shaky legs, Ellen climbed into the truck and into her sleeping bag. Her heart thumped as if she had been running and her center burned as she relived every second of the last few minutes before she finally drifted into a dream of Chance doing it all again.

Had he lost his mind? Chance walked the few paces to his tent. Ellen was driving him beyond reason. He'd always been a sensible adult, one who thought before he acted, yet when he was around Ellen he came unglued. She brushed against him and all he could think of was kissing her, having her. It had become worse when he'd discovered her bare breast. Heaven help him. He'd almost taken her behind the clinic tent. Worse, he still wanted to.

He had to get Ellen out of his system.

Chance slapped at his pants leg in frustration. They were both adults. She had more than proved that with her warm welcome when he'd kissed her. So why couldn't they have a short and satisfying affair while she was here? He would make it clear there would be no ties when the time came for her to leave.

Maybe it was time to stop protecting her. If he didn't do something soon, he wouldn't be able to concentrate on his work. One thing he did know was that he would not be able to push her away any longer. No matter the reason, he wanted her beyond sanity. He would have her.

Come morning, he assigned Ellen to work with Michael as usual. If he'd assigned her to assist him after all this time the others would notice, especially Michael. He wasn't ready to answer questions about his feelings for Ellen.

Throughout the day he would meet Ellen's gaze and she would smile. Once they grabbed for a bandage at the same time. Their hands touched. By his body's reaction he was reverting back to his youth. When they stopped for lunch he sat under a banana tree to eat and watched as Ellen and Karen walked to the truck that doubled as their bedroom. Even Ellen's walk had him turned on.

Michael squatted on his heels beside him. He looked off toward the two women as well. With humor hanging on each word, he said, "I never thought I would have seen it. The untouchable Chance Freeman has fallen hard."

Chance cut his eyes to him. "What does that mean?"

"You have it bad for Ellen."

"You're crazy." Chance picked up a tiny stick and threw it.

"So it's okay if I go after her?"

"You already said she wasn't interested."

"I haven't given her the full court press," Michael said with a smile.

"Leave it alone, Michael," Chance growled.

"Then I suggest you do something about it." Michael looked at the women again.

"You know, it's none of your damn business." Chance didn't need pushing toward something he had every intention of taking care of himself.

Michael chuckled. "No, I guess it isn't but it's nice to see the cool, calm and collected Dr. Freeman squirm." His grin grew larger. "I'll see that the clinic is ready for this afternoon around two."

Michael had been a friend for a number of years and had often listened into the early morning hours to Chance's sad story of his poor choices where women were concerned. More than once they had handled issues having to do with the clinic together. If Michael wasn't such a friend, he would've never gotten away with those remarks about Ellen.

The afternoon work went every bit as well as the morning had. It was dusk when a couple of gunshots rang out in the distance.

"What's that?" Karen asked in alarm.

Michael, appearing unconcerned, continued to store

equipment. "Drug dealers most likely. We've been lucky we haven't heard more shots."

Fifteen minutes later Chance stepped out of the clinic to see a boy of about twelve run into the clearing and stop. He gave the area a wide-eyed look as if searching for something. Ellen slowly approached him from the direction of the truck. She spoke to him.

Chance hurried toward them. As usual she wasn't considering the danger. The boy could be luring her into the jungle. Kidnappings happened often for ransom in this area. She didn't have to step beyond the clearing but a few paces before she wouldn't be seen. Not wanting to spook the boy, Chance slowed as he joined them.

As he came closer the boy said something about his father being shot and asking for her to come help. Chance's heart rate jumped. That had to have been the shots they'd heard. The boy's father must be working with the drug traffickers or had crossed their path.

"Must come," the boy cried. He stepped forward with his hand out as if he were going to take Ellen's.

Chance stepped closer to Ellen and told the child, "You'll need to bring him here."

"Can't. He no walk," the boy said as he looked back toward the opening in the foliage he'd just come out of. "Hurry. Lots blood."

"Then have someone carry him here." Chance made it a firm statement.

The boy looked around as if expecting someone to pop out of the jungle. "No one help. Afraid."

Chance shook his head. "Then I'm sorry."

Ellen gave him a pleading look. "Chance, we have to help."

"My first concern is the staff of this clinic, their safety. Leaving this area would not be safe. The drug traffickers have free rein. We don't even know the boy is telling the truth."

"He die. Please." The boy looked from Ellen to Chance and back again, tears forming in his eyes. "It not far. Promise."

"We have to help him," Ellen begged.

Chance was torn. If it was true he wanted to give the help. But what if it was a trap?

Ellen grabbed his arm and squeezed as she looked at him.

"How far?" Chance asked the boy.

He said a village name Chance wasn't familiar with.

By this time Marco had joined them. Chance looked at him, "How far?"

"Ten-minute walk," Marco said.

"Okay, I'll get supplies and you get my to-go bag." Ellen left before he could say more.

"Should be safe. I send Ricco with you." Marco waved Ricco over.

"Tell me what happened to your father and what part of his body has been hurt," Chance said in rapid Spanish to the boy. Heaven help them if they ran into trouble. He'd let his better judgment be overshadowed by Ellen's beautiful eyes. That unrestricted, forge-forward determination might get them all into trouble. Yet he felt the pull to go as well. There was a patient who needed his help regardless of the danger.

Ellen hurried into the clinic tent and snatched up Chance's bag then headed for the supply van. At first she'd been angry with him for hesitating to help the boy's father. As far as she was concerned, if a person was hurt you had to do whatever was needed to take care of them. Chance's hardline stance didn't impress her. As he spoke more to the boy she saw the sympathy in his eyes. It wasn't that

Chance didn't want to go, it was more that he was responsible for everyone and couldn't make snap decisions. The fact they were going showed that Chance really did care.

Grabbing suture kits, she stuffed them in his bag. She took a couple of bottles of saline out of a storage basket. Finding a spare backpack by the shelf, Ellen dropped the bottles in. She added additional supplies that from her experience might be needed.

Chance entered the van. "I need to get some antibiotics. The boy says his father was shot in the leg."

Ellen stood, letting Chance come behind her. Their bodies bumped in the close quarters. Minutes later, they had what they thought they might need. She left the van first, with him right behind.

"Hand me that backpack," he ordered.

"I can carry it." Ellen offered him his to-go bag instead.

Chance glared at her. "You're not going. Ricco and I will handle this."

"Ricco has medical experience now? How's he supposed to handle a gun at the same time he's helping you? I'm going." Ellen watched his mouth form a tight line. He wasn't going to agree.

"Peter or Karen—"

Ellen huffed. "Karen couldn't keep up the pace and Peter is needed here. We can stand around and argue about this while a man is dying or we can get going." She turned to leave the tent.

He grabbed her under the arm, jerking her round to face him. "You can go *only if* you agree to follow my orders to the letter. No arguments. No going rogue. Either you agree or you stay here. This is still my clinic and my call."

She glared at him and said through her teeth, "I promise to do as you say."

Chance searched her face. "Okay, let's go take care of this patient."

Ellen had no doubt that he didn't like the idea of her going but he recognized he clearly needed her help. She adjusted the pack on her back as he slung the strap of his bag across his chest. At a lope he crossed the clearing and Ellen followed close behind.

"You ready?" Chance asked Ricco, who nodded. "Ellen, I want you between Ricco and me."

She moved into position.

To the boy Chance said, "Take us to your father."

The boy dipped his head under a large leaf and moved into the jungle. Chance followed with Ellen and seconds behind her Ricco. The path was little more than a foot wide. She wouldn't have even said there was one if she hadn't been behind Chance. As they walked he held leaves and vines back. She accepted them and did the same for Ricco.

"Stay close and don't speak unless necessary," Chance hissed over his shoulder.

Underfoot was dark packed dirt crisscrossed with roots. Her boots were so new they didn't make the best hiking wear. A couple of times she caught a toe on a root but righted herself before she tripped. Once Ricco caught her arm before she fell.

Another time Chance stopped and she bumped into his back. He cautiously looked around. The boy was standing a few feet in front of him, looking down the path. They waited then moved forward at a slower pace. Finally, they broke out of the jungle into an open space next to a creek with five small huts. The roofs were pieces of tin or plastic tarps peaked just enough for rain to roll off. The walls were little more than uneven boards wired together to form a square. The boy led them through knee-high grass to one of the stacks closest to the water.

He stepped through an opening into a hut that had no door. Chance and she followed. Ricco stayed on guard outside. The sun was almost over the horizon, making it dark inside. The boy told a woman there that he had brought the doctors.

Ellen could make out someone lying on an old mattress on the dirt floor across the room. Chance was already stepping that way and Ellen joined him.

"We have to have some light here." He sounded exasperated as he went down on his knees to speak to the barely conscious man.

Ellen pulled off the backpack, opened it and removed a flashlight. Clicking it on, she held it over Chance's head.

He glanced up. "Well done, Ellen. I should have known you'd consider the details."

She couldn't help but be pleased with his praise.

"Can you point the light toward the left some?"

Ellen did as he requested. From her vantage point she could see the dark-skinned man was maybe thirty, dressed in a torn shirt with baggy shorts. One leg of the pants was pulled high on his leg. Below that on his thigh were two dirty rags covered in blood. Even if they could help him, fighting infection would be the larger battle.

"Look at this," Chance said with revulsion in his words.

She understood his feelings. "Two shots. He really needs to be in a hospital."

"Agreed, but that would be in a perfect world and this isn't one. Nearest hospital is too far away and he would never make it, even if he would allow us to take him."

Ellen leaned closer for a better look. "He's lost a lot of blood. He needs a transfusion."

"I'm O. Have you ever done a transfusion outside a hospital?"

"No."

"Then I'll set that up and you can take care of the wounds while I'm giving blood. Ever removed a bullet?"

She gave him a wry smile. "I saw it done during emergency rotation."

"Can you handle it?"

"Sure I can. So if I understand this right, you're going to lie around while I do all the work?"

"Funny lady." Chance reached for his pack.

She came down on her knees beside him.

Chance called to the boy to come and hold the flashlight and asked the woman to get them some hot water. He then prepared a syringe of antibiotic and injected it into the man's arm. "It'll be too little, too late, but it's better than nothing."

Ellen could identify with his frustration. She pulled the saline bottles out of the backpack as Chance removed supplies from his bag. Slipping on gloves, she lifted the bandage off the upper hole in the man's leg. It was still oozing. She opened up some four-by-fours and placed them over it, then gave the same attention to the other one. As Ellen worked Chance was busy setting up an IV line. With efficiency and precision that she admired, he'd already inserted the needle into the man's arm.

Chance spoke to the boy again and he dashed out the door. The woman arrived with the water. Ellen continued to clean around the first wound. The boy returned with a wooden chair that had seen better days and a lantern. Chance placed the chair close to the mattress. Ellen took the lantern, situating it so she could get the most out of its light.

"I'm ready for you to finish this IV," Chance said.

"Let me change gloves." Ellen stripped off the ones she'd been wearing and pulled on clean ones. She moved close to Chance. Taking his arm under hers, she held his steady and began pressing on the bend in his elbow for a good vein. She was close enough to catch the natural scent of him.

"You know, you really are beautiful."

She glanced up then down again. "You're not already light-headed, are you?" With a firm, steady push she inserted the large IV needle into his arm. "Hand me one of those tape strips."

"No, just speaking the truth." He handed her a strip from the ones he'd placed on the backpack. "This isn't your first stick. Nicely done."

"Thank you. Yes, I've done a few in my time." She looked him straight in the eyes. "But I'm always open to a first time in other areas." His eyes widened slightly before he started pumping his fist and blood flowed to their patient.

"You'd better get busy on those holes or you'll be wasting my blood."

"I'm on it." She removed her gloves and replaced them with clean ones again. "I'll have them taken care of and get back to you in a minute."

Ellen carefully cleaned around the surface of the first wound. She was going to have to remove the bullet and not damage the nearby artery while doing it. Even in the best of situations that would still have a degree of difficulty. Under these conditions that was upped a hundred times. Ellen counted on her skill to save this man, if not her experience.

Locating large tweezers, she cleaned the blood away and went after the bullet. She pursed her lips tightly as she continued to search. Finding the bullet, she grabbed it and pulled it out. The wound bled anew. She dropped the bullet to the floor and snatched some four-by-fours and placed them over the hole.

"Nice job, Doctor."

"Thanks, but I have to stop this bleeding. Could you apply pressure while I get the sutures ready?"

"Sure. Now I'm assisting you."

She glanced at him. "Problem with that?"

"Not at all." After she'd helped him pull on a glove, he put two fingers in the center of the pads.

Minutes later Ellen had the wound sutured closed. She checked on Chance as she worked. She didn't need him passing out. He seemed comfortable. The entire time she worked she was conscious of him watching her.

As she applied the final piece of tape to the bandage Chance said, "You handled yourself well, Dr. Cox."

"Thank you. How're you doing?" She took the patient's vital signs. He was stable, but barely.

"I think I'm about at the end of my giving. Head's a little light."

"Well, let me try to stand and I'll see about you." She pushed up but her knees were stiff and didn't want to move.

"Give me your hand and I'll pull."

She took his hand. It was a struggle but she finally made it to her feet.

"Walk around a minute and get some feeling back into your legs."

Ellen took his suggestion and made a couple of circles around the shack.

Returning to Chance, she removed the needle and applied a pressure bandage. "Now, sit there for a while. I don't need two patients. I'll have to admit this is out of my usual wheelhouse. Even in a clinic in the middle of New York City, what we have done here is over the top."

"If it makes you feel any better, this is a little extreme for me as well."

"Thanks for that. I thought you might remind me again that I shouldn't be here."

"I only acted that way because I was afraid that you had bitten off more than you could chew. These conditions are harsh."

What he didn't say was that today was an example of that. She had a patient waiting and couldn't worry about that now. Going down on her knees again, she started caring for the last bullet wound. With the lower one, the bullet had gone clean through. Working as efficiently as possible with the few supplies as she had left, she closed the wounds Done, she started cleaning up.

In all the medical work she had ever done she'd never felt better or more confident about herself than she did at this moment. This work was what she had been born for.

She looked at him. "We're not all the hothouse flowers you think we are."

"I know that now. You've more than proved it." Chance looked around the shack. "It seems we're here for the night. We need to keep an eye on him." He nodded toward the injured man.

Ellen placed a hand on their patient's head. "Infection is our enemy now. And you don't need to do any activity for a while either."

Chance looked in the direction of the woman and boy, who waited in the corner in what was nothing more than a makeshift kitchen. There was a small table and a bench with a shelf above it. A bucket sat on the bench. Chance spoke to the boy, "Can you find us something to sleep on? A blanket for your father? Something to eat?"

"Si." The boy left and the woman went out the door behind him.

Chance stood and walked to the doorway. Ellen joined him. Chance spoke to Ricco. He nodded and move to the corner of the building, his gun at the ready. She and Chance continued to stand there. The night sounds were almost overwhelming as animals as well as bugs communicated.

"This is an amazing country," Ellen said. "I know why you keep coming back."

"It is."

She looked at him. "You love it here, don't you?"

"If I said I didn't, you would call me a liar."

Ellen smiled. "That I would."

The boy returned carrying a rolled-up tarp. They followed him inside. He placed it on the floor. "Sleep." He pointed to it.

Chance chuckled. "All the comforts of home."

"Better than the dirt." Ellen sat on it with her legs crossed.

"Do you ever see the negative in anything?" Chance asked, taking the chair again.

"Sometimes but it's better to see the positive because the negative is usually far too obvious."

The woman came in holding two banana leaves. She handed one to her and the other to Chance. Ellen had never seen anything like it.

"Pulled pork and vegetables. It's cooked in the ground. You'll like it." Chance picked up a bite between his thumb and forefinger and put it in his mouth.

Ellen wasn't so eager. She looked at it more closely in the dim light then moved it around with a tip of a finger.

"This is the first time I've seen you squeamish about something. You need to eat."

"I'm just not sure about this. I usually have my food on a plate."

Chance chuckled. "Just pretend that you're at a baseball game and you're having a hotdog."

"My father has box seats for the Mets and a cook comes in."

Chance's fingers stopped halfway to his mouth. "Just who is your father?"

"Robert Cox." Even in the low light she could see Chance's eyes widen.

"As in Cox Media."

"Yes. That's my father's company."

"So why in the hell are you down here? You don't need the money or even to work."

She glowered at him. "I'm a doctor because I want to help people. And today shows that I'm needed. Even by you." In a show of defiance, she picked up a finger full of food and plopped it into her mouth. "That's good."

The boy came in again, this time with two bottled drinks. He gave them each one.

Chance said, "No matter how far out of civilization you get, soda companies are there. Thank goodness. We don't need to drink the water."

Ellen finished off her meal and stood. "Let me have those." Chance handed her his leaf and bottle. "I'll put this away and then check the patient. You need to sleep. Work on building new blood cells."

"Yes, ma'am."

"No argument?" Ellen looked at him.

"Nope."

"We really have gone into a different world." She placed the stuff she held on the bench then stepped over to her patient. He seemed comfortable enough. There was a low fever but that was expected. "We'll need to get him out of here and to a hospital tomorrow."

"Agreed," Chance said as he lay out on the tarp. "Come on, you need some rest as much as I do."

Ellen stretched out beside him, leaving as much space as possible between them. She put her arm under her head, trying to get comfortable.

"Come over here," Chance said. "You can use my shoulder for a pillow."

The tarp made a crinkling sound as she shifted closer. She laid her head on his broad shoulder. He moved his arm around her and his hand settled on her waist.

In a sleepy voice he said, "I've dreamed of sleeping with you but never in a shack in the middle of the jungle."

Ellen rolled toward him and her arm went across his waist. She didn't care where it was, just that she was near him.

CHAPTER FIVE

CHANCE ROSE A couple of times during the night to check on their patient. Each time Ellen curled into the warm spot he had left. When he returned she moaned her appreciation as he took her into his arms again. That kind of treatment he could get used to.

He looked out the doorway at the full moon. It was well after midnight. Their patient had spiked a fever. After giving him another dose of antibiotics, Chance used a four-by-four to bathe his head. Under these conditions there wasn't much more he could do. He joined Ellen again.

"How's he doing?" she murmured.

"Fever's down. Go back to sleep."

"Next time I'll get up."

He pulled her close again. "Deal."

The sky was still more dark than light when Chance was shaken awake. "Must go," the boy said in a low urgent whisper. "Now."

Chance was instantly alert.

The boy was already picking up Chance's to-go bag and putting things in it. "Bad men come. Must hide."

Chance stood and helped Ellen to her feet.

"They find you, they kill you." The boy didn't slow down.

His statement propelled Chance into action. "Ellen,

make sure we have everything picked up that might indicate who we are. Leave nothing behind." He grabbed her backpack and finished putting their things, even the paper covers, into the pack. Done, he zippered it up.

"What's going on?" Ellen looked around as if unsure what to do first.

"Drug traffickers. They're looking for our patient over there. If they find us they'll kill me and ransom you. If you're lucky."

"What about our patient?" She started toward the man.

"We've done all we can for him. Now we have to take care of ourselves." He thrust the backpack at her. "Put it on. Do exactly as I say. No more questions." He took his pack from the boy and pulled the strap over his shoulder. "Let's go."

"Ricco?" she asked.

The boy went to the door and stopped. "He leave when the men come close. Hide. Then warn doctors." The boy waved them on. Instead of heading across the grassy field, the boy led them to the edge of the jungle. There he went into a squat. Chance followed suit and pulled Ellen down beside him. The boy searched the area.

There was a stillness in the air as if nature was waiting for something to happen. No birds chattered in the trees or monkeys swung from limb to limb. Seconds later voices broke the silence. The boy put his finger across his mouth. They waited, waited. The sounds came no closer.

The boy, followed by Ellen and then Chance ran stooped over around the edge of the field for a time until they ducked into the foliage near a large banyan tree. At almost a run they headed down a path that was harder to follow than the one they had been on the day before.

They had been moving at a fast pace for about ten minutes when Ellen tripped and went down on her hands. Chance grabbed her by the waist and pulled her to her feet.

"Are you all right?" he whispered close to her ear.

She nodded.

Chance looked at the boy, who had paused. He waved them forward.

"We have to move." Chance took Ellen's hand and started after the boy.

As they ran Chance tried to push the leaves back so they wouldn't slap Ellen in the face but wasn't always successful. She kept up despite the difference in their size and the fact she was wearing chunky boots. A few minutes later the boy pulled to a stop and squatted on his heels.

Ellen took a seat on a large root. Strands of hair hung around her face. Her cheeks were bright red. Her deep breathing filled the air along with his and the boy's.

Standing, the boy said quietly, "I must go to my father. You follow path to river, then go down river to Saba." The boy headed up the path the way they had come.

"He's leaving us?" Ellen whispered in disbelief.

"Yes. He'll be missed and we'll be in more danger."

"Won't they know we have been there when they see his father?"

"Maybe they won't look that closely or hopefully they don't even check the shack." Chance offered her his hand and she took it. "We need to put as much distance between us and them as we can."

He hurried down the path but not at a run and Ellen kept pace with him. As they went the birds started to call at each other and the animals scurried off. At least the jungle was accepting them. If the traffickers were close and they heard no noise they would know where he and Ellen were.

They had been walking for about an hour when Chance stopped and led Ellen off the path. Stepping through the vegetation about ten feet, he found a large fig tree that would give them plenty of cover.

"Why're we stopping?"

"You need to rest." He looked around. "Hell, I need to rest. Take a seat."

Ellen pulled off her pack and dropped it to the ground. Satisfied that they were out of sight of the path, Chance joined her on the ground.

"Any way you have some food in that bag?"

He grinned. "As a matter of fact I do. Two or three breakfast bars."

"That's what I love, a man who's prepared for a quick run through the jungle."

Chance chuckled and started searching though his bag. No one was prepared for this situation but he didn't want to scare her by saying that. He pulled out a bar. Tearing it open, he handed her half of it. "It's more like a man who has had to go a day without a meal."

"Do you know where we are?"

This was a conversation he wasn't looking forward to having. It would go one of two ways: she would panic or she would take it in her stride. So far Ellen had been a good sport but this was more than they both had bargained for when he'd agreed to go help the boy's father. "Three days is my best guess if we don't run into trouble."

"Three days!" Her voice rose. Birds squawked and flew away.

"Shush, we don't know who else is nearby."

Ellen's brows grew together and she looked around with concern. "Sorry."

"Just be careful from now on. We have to walk and it won't be an easy one. Even following the river, we have to circle any villages we come to. We don't know who we can trust."

"We really are in a mess. I'm sorry I insisted that we

help the father." She took a bite of the bar. "Now I've put us in danger."

"It didn't take much for me to agree. Let's not worry about it. We need to make plans. First, we have to conserve what food we have. Which consists of two and a half bars. We'll need water." He was now talking more to himself than her.

"We have the two saline bottles. We can fill them up at the river."

"No, we mustn't drink the water unless we have no other choice. The chance of getting a parasite is too great. We'll collect rain water. We'll just have to make do until it rains." Thankfully it did that almost daily.

By the deflated look on Ellen's face he suspected she was thirsty now but she didn't say anything.

"Do you have any idea where we are?"

"Some but we're far deeper in-country and north than I've ever been." Maybe he shouldn't be quite so truthful with her but he couldn't bring himself to lie either. He finished his half of the bar and put the paper in his bag. "We'd better get going."

They both stood. He gave her a hand signal to stay and stepped out to check the path then waved her to join him. Chance offered his hand. Ellen took it. She trusted him to get them out of this. He just hoped he'd earned her faith.

Ellen realized she was in over her head this time. She'd done what her had father worried would happen. Taken a risk. It was starting to take a great deal of effort to contain her fear. The pace Chance set had her feet aching and her body sweating. By the time the rush of the river could be heard the sun was high in the sky.

Her mouth was desert dry and her clothes stuck to her skin. She couldn't remember being more miserable but she refused to say anything or ask to slow down. There was no way she would be responsible for putting them in more danger. She'd already placed them in enough.

Chance stopped. "Stay here. I'll be right back."

She nodded but didn't like the idea of being left. By the sound of the water the river was around the next bend. Surely Chance wouldn't be gone long. When he was no longer in sight panic pushed its way into her chest. She looked up the path from the direction they had come. Then back to where Chance had gone. What if something happened to him and she was left out here alone? What if he got hurt and needed her? What if those men found him? Why didn't he hurry?

With a flow of relief that had to equal the river in size, she saw Chance coming back.

When he joined her again he gave her a searching look. "You okay? Hear something?"

She gave him a weak smile. "I'm fine. Everything is fine."

"That might be stretching the truth. River's right ahead. There's a path running beside it. We'll use it but we'll have to be careful not to run into anyone."

"You lead, I follow."

"When we get down a way we'll stop and cool off for a while."

"Gives me something to look forward to."

Chance started down the path. "I'll give you this, Ellen Cox, you're a trouper."

The path widened and she walked beside him. "You might want to save that praise until you see how I do over the next few of days."

He took her hand and squeezed it. "We'll make it."

Ellen couldn't contain the "Aw" that came out at the sight of the river. It was breathtaking. The water flowing over the white rounded boulders whooshed and boiled as it made its way to the coast. The contrast of the vivid vegetation framing it and the blue of the sky above made for a perfect picture. If it hadn't been for the situation they were in she would have sworn she was in paradise.

Chance let go of her hand and stood beside her. "It's just one of the many things I love about this country, the beauty."

They started moving again. "Still, you've had a hard time dealing with all the needs you see and keeping the hospital going."

"I have to admit that the struggle to retain staff, find funding and most of all making a real difference here has started to eat away at me."

It was the first time she'd heard him really share his feelings about anything personal. "So your plan was to discourage help when it shows up?"

As they walked along the path beside the river he pointed down, "Watch the rocks. We don't need a twisted ankle to deal with."

A couple of minutes went by as they maneuvered over a narrow, difficult area. Back on a wider section, Ellen said, "You didn't answer my question."

"I don't discourage people from coming. In fact, I encourage them. We need the help down here."

"I didn't get that kind of welcome."

"Only because you reminded me of my ex-wife at first, then because you didn't. I wasn't sure you could handle this type of work. I was concerned for your safety. Still am." He took her hand and helped her down over a slippery area.

It was nice to have someone care but she was a survivor. She'd learned that when her mother had died and during those days in the hospital. "But there's more to it."

It took him a second to answer. "I was attracted to you and I didn't want to be."

"Why's that such a bad thing?"

"Because I have nothing real to offer you."

Before she could get him to clarify that statement he said, "Here's a good place to rest." The river slowed and created a pool. "I'll keep watch while you clean up. Just be sure not to swallow any water despite how temping it might be."

Ellen crouched beside the river. She must look a fright. Cupping her hands, she splashed water onto her face. She did it again, rubbing her hands down her cheeks, and was amazed at the dirt that came off. The water felt wonderful. Cool and refreshing. Cupping another handful of liquid, she ran her hand along the back of her neck. Now, if she could just have a drink.

She sat on a rock and started working with her boot-lace. "I'm going to take my boots off and cool off my feet for a second."

"No. Don't." Chance's tone was sharp. "You won't be able to get them back on because your feet will be so swollen. Hopefully, we'll be somewhere tonight where you can remove them."

Ellen started re-lacing her boot. So much for the pleasure of having water run over her throbbing feet. Done, she stood. "Your turn."

Chance stepped to the river and began cleaning himself. As she expected, he poured and splashed the water into his hair. He slung his head back. His hair curled and dripped around the collar of his safari shirt. In an odd way he belonged to the wild uncertain world around them.

While he was doing that she checked up and down the path. Pulling her band from her hair, she let it fall then gathered it again, working to get all the loose strands back under control.

The shrill call of a bird had her jerking around to search the area behind them. She looked back at Chance. He was on guard as well.

Stepping away from the river, he picked up his bag and came to her. "Come on, we're both tired and jumpy. We need to rest. Get out of the heat. We'll start again in an hour or so." He pushed leaves of rhododendron the size of a man and vines out of the away, putting distance between them and the path. They soon came to a banyan tree.

"This should do. We have cover here." He bent over and weaved his way between the roots that grew almost head high in abundance around the tree.

Ellen followed.

Chance put his satchel on the ground, lay down and used the bag as a pillow. Ellen took the space beside him, doing the same with her backpack. After they were settled and still, the birds started talking again. She looked up into the tree, catching glimpses of sky through the thick canopy.

"Chance," she whispered.

"Mmm?"

"Tell me about your ex."

He rolled his head toward her and opened one eye. "Why do you want to know about her?"

There was a hint of pain in his voice. She must have destroyed him.

"Because I think she is part of the reason why you've been trying to stop anything from happening between us."

Chance looked away. She wasn't sure if his eyes were closed or if he was staring off into the distance.

He took a deep breath and let it out slowly. "I met her at a fund-raiser. She was all about looks, which worked because she had them. In spades. Blonde, blue-eyed, leggy."

Ellen's lips tightened. *Like her.*

"I fell for her right away. She liked the good things in life and she was more than glad to hitch a ride with me. What she didn't bargain on was living in Honduras. She came from a middle-class background where they camped on vacation and didn't have the comforts of high living so I thought she would do fine down here, especially staying at the resort. It didn't take her long to start complaining about the heat, the bugs, the rain and most of all having to spend the day by herself. She wanted nothing to do with the clinic. There wasn't enough to do and she was lonely."

Ellen could hear the disgust and disappointment in his voice.

"One of my buddies from med school came down to work for six weeks. She had been so unhappy that when she started spending time with Jim and smiling again I was glad. Suddenly she wanted to come out with us and help at the clinic. I thought it was a good idea. The more she saw maybe the more she'd want to help. Yeah, right. It turned out they were having an affair. He was from an old Boston family with the name and money to please her. When he left, she went with him." The last he all but spit out.

"I'm sorry that happened to you."

"It was a long time ago. I've moved on."

Ellen had never known a person more in denial. "You do know I'm nothing like her?"

"Yeah, I figured that out pretty quickly." There was a contrite note in his voice. "I was tough on you there at first."

"You think?"

He smiled slightly.

"So those question and comments about Michael and me was you being jealous?"

"I wouldn't say that."

She leaned over him and looked into his eyes. "I would."

Their gazes held for a long time before he said, "Lie back, Dr. Cox, and get some rest. You're going to need it."

Ellen did as he asked with a grin on her face. He cared

far more than he let on. Could she have a relationship with Chance and still maintain the freedom she'd fought so hard to gain? From what she'd learned about him, he had a strong need to protect. Could she handle that?

The sounds of the birds as they took flight from the top of the trees woke her. Chance rolled over her and put a finger to her lips. His body remained rigid and still. Seconds later the voices of males speaking in Spanish reached her ears. They were on the path. She only caught a few words because the dialect was so different. Words like "find" and "American" she understood.

They were looking for them!

Chance saw the fear in Ellen's eyes. Her body trembled beneath him. She'd heard the men. They were in more danger than he'd believed. The drug traffickers were determined to find them. Ellen's eyes were wide with terror. She squirmed as if wanting to run.

He brushed his lips over hers as he shook his head. Bringing his hand to her cheek, he held her so that he could deepen the kiss. Ellen opened. Her tongue mated with his. Fingers weaved into the hair at the nape of his neck and her body softened. She kissed him with the passion of a person hanging on to life. An arm came down to his waist then pushed under his shirt and grasped his back.

Heaven help him, Chance wanted her. Here. In the jungle. On the ground. Beneath this tree. But he couldn't. He must keep her safe.

His lips remained on hers as he listened for the men. They had moved on but they were going the same way as them. They would have to wait here and let them get further down river then cross over. Find somewhere to hole up for the night. It would mean more time in the jungle but getting Ellen back in one piece would be worth it.

She quit kissing him. He opened his eyes. Hers were fixed on him. He put his finger to her lips. She kissed it. Thankfully the panic had cleared from her eyes. Passion and questions filled them now.

"Shh."

She nodded. He rolled off her and sat up. She did the same. They waited there, just listening, for what seemed like an eternity. The birds settled again. All he could make out was the usual jungle sounds.

Standing, he extended his hand and helped her to her feet. He put his finger to his lips again then gently pushed the undergrowth back as they made progress toward the river. Ellen was glued to his back as if they were one. He paused and carefully searched the area before they stepped out onto the path.

Using a low voice, he said, "We have to cross the river and find somewhere to stay the night. Maybe they'll give up by tomorrow."

She nodded.

"We need to do it here. I'm afraid to go downstream any farther. We'll cross at those rocks." He pointed down the river just below the pool. "Guess what? You get to take those boots off after all. We don't want to get them wet or they'll be even harder to walk in. Tie the laces together and put them around your neck."

Ellen did as he instructed without question. Minutes later they were ready to go. Chance led her across some rocks and down into the water and up again. There was a section where the water was moving fast between two large rocks close to the bank. It was moving rapidly enough that Ellen wouldn't be strong enough to walk through it without assistance.

"I'll step over then help you though." Chance didn't wait for a response. They had to get out of the open. There was no way of knowing if the men would come back this way. He held on to the rock and put a foot into the gushing water. Secure, he took a long step, making it across the flow. He offered his arm to Ellen. She grasped his forearm and he hers. He swung her more than helped her over the divide. She now stood a little in front of him.

In his peripheral vision he saw a flash of color. He pushed Ellen into the deeper water surrounding a large rock. When he did so he slipped. He was headed down the river and right into the sight of the men looking for them.

His bag strap held him back. Seconds later he felt a tug across his chest.

"Help," Ellen whispered close to his ear.

Using a foot, Chance pushed against a rock beneath the water and back toward her. He did it once more. Now at least half of his body was behind the rock, lying over Ellen's. She held tightly to the strap, pulling him against her chest. The water tugged at him as it flowed over his legs but Ellen held steady. They stayed in that position without daring to look to see where the men were for a long time. The shadows were long on their side of the river before Chance had the nerve to lean forward. Scanning the area, he saw no sign of human life.

He worked to find adequate footing then managed to get turned around and to the bank. Ellen took his hand and he brought her over to join him. They climbed out of the water and moved into the vegetation. Sitting, he said, "Thanks for saving my butt back there."

"Think nothing of it." She sounded exhausted.

"When did you see—?"

"About the same time you did. I couldn't think of anything to do but hold on."

"You did well." What he didn't want to tell her was that they had bigger problems now. Like it was getting dark and they had no safe place to stay for the night. "Let's get our boots on. We need to get moving. The good news is that they were headed upstream so the chances of us meeting them again is slim."

"So there'll be no more distraction kisses?"

"I hope not."

"Shame, I rather enjoyed it."

He grinned. "I did too. Get your shoes on. We need to get going."

"I'm afraid they're wet." Ellen dumped water out of one of hers.

"We'll have to wear them anyway."

They both had their boots on and were ready to go in a few minutes. Once again Chance led, pushing plants out of the way. It was rough walking but they made headway. He almost kissed the ground when they came to a path. Keeping the sound of the river to his right, he could be sure they were still headed toward the coast.

Now to find a place for them to stay for the night. They were both soaking wet. He was starting to chap and Ellen must be also. But still no complaint. He shook his head. The woman with hot pink fingernails had just saved his life. Who would have thought?

Where did she find that fortitude? In his experience with women they would have broken down long ago. As the daughter of Robert Cox she'd grown up in a privileged home. He couldn't imagined her having done anything that would prepare her for this type of undertaking. It was nice to have someone he wasn't having to reassure all the time. A partner in the effort.

They walked about an hour without seeing any obvious good place for shelter. Under the tree canopy it was almost dark. He had to find something soon. As if in answer to his prayer, a giant kapok tree came into view. It was so large that its trunk and roots created a cave of sorts. They had just made it to the tree when rain started to fall. Ellen stood with her mouth open, letting the drops off a leaf fall into her mouth. He wished he could let her continue but they had to see to their needs first.

"Get the bottles and put them where they'll collect water. I'll make sure we don't have any company inside this tree. Then we need to get out of these clothes and shoes. We can't take a chance on a fire but we do need to give our bodies relief from the damp."

Chance left her to see about the drinking water while he checked out the tree. There was just enough room for them to both lie down. At least it was dry. He returned outside and found a banana tree and started stripping leaves from it. He would use them to clean out any ants or spiders that might want to share their room. They couldn't afford to be bitten.

He'd just finished and had their bags inside when Ellen joined him, soaking wet. She had one full bottle of water in her hand.

"I poured what I had in one. I'll go out after the other in a few minutes. Have some." She handed it to him like she was giving a Christmas present. "It's wonderful."

Chance gladly took a swallow. And another, before handing it back to her. "Drink all you can so we can fill it up again."

She did as he said and passed it to him once more.

"I think we're safe here so we need to get out of these clothes. There's a root we can hang them on. They won't dry completely but it's better than nothing." Chance started unbuttoning his shirt. He couldn't help but watch Ellen pull her T-shirt over her head. Why couldn't there be more light? Beneath she wore a sports bra.

"Please, don't look at me like that. I'm not used to undressing in front of a man."

Chance unbuckled his belt, bent over and removed his boots then dropped his pants. "You certainly have nothing to be ashamed of. You're amazing."

"From what I can see of you, you're not so bad yourself. So you're a briefs guy. And I would have said boxers."

She'd given thought to what type of underwear he wore? He rather liked that idea.

Ellen sat on a banana leaf and removed her boots then stood. The sound of a zipper drew Chance's attention away from hanging clothes. In the dim light he could see a strip of white bikini panties. Once again he had to remind himself to focus on keeping them alive instead of his baser desires.

"Hand me those," he said in a gruff voice.

She gave him her pants.

"We need to go through our packs and see what we have that we can use to gather food and attend to our feet. I don't know about you but mine feel like shriveled-up prunes." The job needed to be done but it would also keep his mind off the half-naked woman sharing a tree bedroom in the middle of nowhere with him. It should have been the stuff that dreams were made of. Instead they were in a nightmare.

He'd worked hard all day to sound upbeat and not to show his fear and concern. Gut-wrenching anxiety filled him any time he let himself think about their situation. People with guns were after them, they were dehydrated, had no real food, their feet were blistered, they were insect bitten, and exhausted. He just couldn't let on to Ellen how dire their situation was.

She sat on a banana leaf again and opened her backpack. She started laying things out. When she found the flashlight she start to turn it on.

"Wait until we have everything out so we don't waste the batteries."

"It's so wet it might not work."

"It's the kind sealed for water. It should be fine."

She went back to digging in the pack. "What's this?" She held a rag with its ends tied. She opened it carefully. It was food like the boy had bought them last night.

"The boy must have put it in there when he was packing things up."

"I don't care how it got here, I'm just grateful to have it. I'm starving." She handed one to him.

They stopped what they were doing and took a moment to eat. Neither said anything about saving some but they only ate a little. Chance gave his back to her and she put them both back into the rag and tied it.

"Okay, what else do we have?" she asked.

Most of what they had was medical supplies, which did them little good for food or drink.

"Let me see that light. I want to look at your feet."

"Why, Doctor, that's a kinky idea." Ellen brought her feet around in his direction.

"Funny. You keep that up and I might tickle them." Chance shined the light on her feet. He wanted to cry. They had blisters and were bleeding in some places. "I have some antibiotic ointment I'm going to put on these. Why didn't you say something?"

"We couldn't stop, could we?"

"No."

"Then what was the point? I'm sure yours are just as bad. Finish up with mine and then I'll see to yours."

He gently applied the ointment to her feet but it wouldn't really help much. The air and time out of her boots were the best healer. "Before you do mine, let me go out and see to the water." Chance picked up the bottle and headed outside. He soon returned to find her repacking their bags.

"It's your turn." Chance wiped as much dirt off his feet as possible and sat down to let her examine them.

Her hands were gentle as she checked each angry spot and applied the cream. She was an above-average doctor.

"We're both in sad shape but we'll survive. My father will never believe this. I'll be lucky if he lets me out of town again."

Chance placed banana leaves so that they had a bed of sorts. He put his bag and her pack on it and lay back. Patting the area beside him, he said, "Join me."

Ellen did but didn't touch him.

He clicked off the flashlight. "Would you mind keeping me warm?"

She placed her head on his shoulder and wrapped an arm around his waist. Shifting, she got comfortable and he became uncomfortable. He could so easily roll over and make love to her but he was bone weary and she could only be just as tired. They needed their rest more than release.

"These banana leaves make you think a dirty tarp isn't so bad."

Chance chuckled and kissed her temple. "You never cease to amaze me."

The soft sound of her even breathing brought the only feeling of peace he'd found all day.

CHAPTER SIX

THEY HAD BEEN walking since sunrise and Ellen's feet were already screaming. Even with the attention Chance had given them they'd still had to go back into damp leather boots. It hadn't been a pleasant experience. To have a thick, dry pair of socks would have been wonderful. But that was only a fantasy.

Ellen had wanted to work in a developing country but this was more than she had planned on. Sleeping in a tree in only her underwear hadn't been a scenario she would have imagined. She had slept, though. Exhausted from hiking, swimming and raw fear, she'd been fast asleep as soon as her head had snuggled into Chance's shoulder. Despite her lack of clothing, she'd been warm the entire night nestled against Chance.

Sometime she had been jerked awake by the sound of a wild animal growling.

"Shush, sweetheart. He's a long way off. Go back to sleep." Chance's hand had caressed her hip and waist.

For once she'd appreciated his protection. She hadn't questioned further and had soon been asleep again. How did Chance do that? Make her feel secure by just being there? She'd been consumed by fear the day before. She'd run down a path in the jungle without question because

Chance had said that was what they needed to do, and had been confident he would take care of her.

He'd distracted her by kissing her when she'd been so sure the bad men just feet away would find them. The kiss had started out as something to help her keep quiet but had turned into a passionate meeting of lips, as all of her and Chance's kisses had. Her distress had disappeared with only a touch from him.

The pinnacle of her terror had been those seconds before she'd wrapped her hands around his bag strap and pulled him back against her. It had taken all her strength but she'd managed by sheer determination. Her heart had been in her throat and there had been a roaring sound in her ears. Losing him hadn't been something she would even consider. If he had been washed away and the drug traffickers had seen him they would have shot at him. She couldn't let that happen. After they'd climbed out of the river the look on Chance's face had aid he was proud of her. She'd wanted to dance a gig in happiness that they'd been alive but she'd been afraid they'd be seen or heard.

Ellen watched Chance walking ahead of her a few paces. He was confident and watchful at the same time. He had to move a leaf or push away a vine more often than she because he was taller. His clothes clung to his body in the tropical dampness. Occasionally he pushed his hair back with a hand when he glanced over his shoulder to check on her.

She and Chance had become a true partnership through this ordeal. He was no longer pushing her away. Last night he'd trusted her to see to something as important as the water. He saw her as a competent person, something that her father would never open his eyes to. Someone who could take care of herself. For that alone she adored Chance. She looked at his broad shoulders and the back of his handsome head. Her heart was full.

Sometime later Chance called for a rest stop. They shared a bottle of water. There was little better than the feel of the liquid going down her parched throat.

"I'd like half a bar, if that's okay?" Ellen said.

"Sure. I'll join you." Chance pulled a food bar out of a side pocket of his bag. Opening and breaking it, he gave her a piece.

Ellen found a seat on a nearby root. "So how long should it take us to get to Saba?"

"Maybe tomorrow evening if we're lucky. If we can keep the same pace as we have been. How are your feet?"

"Much like yours, I imagine."

His chuckle was a dry one. "My boots are more broken in than yours. I'm sure your feet are dying to get out and dry out."

"It may be a long time before I can wear open-toed shoes again. I'm pretty sure I'm going to lose some skin."

Chance sat beside her and took one of her hands in his. He stroked a fingertip much like the Honduran girls had. Her nails were no longer neatly polished. A number of them were broken and chipped. Dirt circled the cuticles. Under any other circumstances she wouldn't have let him look at them. Now she was just too tired to argue.

"I'm sorry." He sounded sad.

"For what?"

"Your nails."

"I thought you hated them. Thought they were…frivolous."

"No. They're one of the nicest things about you."

"Really? You could have fooled me. You acted like I had committed a crime when I brought out my polish."

He kissed a knuckle. "Yeah, but you made those girls' day." He kissed another. "I couldn't fault you for that." He touched his lips to a different knuckle. "When we get out of this I'll see that you get a day of pampering at the resort. Including a manicure and pedicure."

"What about you? You'll deserve something."

"I'll get to enjoy you." He gave her a quick kiss.

Warmth seeped through her that had nothing to do with the steamy weather or the sun beaming down on them. They still hadn't had that talk he had promised but she was going to see to it that they did.

"Come on, it's time for some more walking." Chance stood and helped her up.

It was around noon when the sound of the river grew louder.

"We're getting closer to the river," Ellen said.

"Yes. I think this path leads to a ford. It's time we crossed back over," Chance said. "Wait here and I'll check it out."

Her chest tightened. "I'm going with you. I don't like it when you leave."

He regarded her a moment. "You know, that's the first complaint you've made since we started this trek."

"Complaining does no good. I learned that a long time ago." That lesson had been clear when she'd been trapped in a car with her mother and later in the hospital. Even with her father she'd found out that she didn't make headway by complaining. It hadn't been until she'd forced the issue by coming here that she'd made a step away from him.

Chance took one of her hands in his. "Why now?"

"Because I'm afraid that something will happen and you won't come back." Was that how her father felt? This was the fear he knew when he thought of losing her?

"I won't be out of your sight two minutes. Promise."

She tapped her wristwatch. "I'm going to time you."

"I expected nothing less. While I'm gone think about

what you want to do when we get back to the resort. I want to hear every detail." He hurried off.

She was so busy making plans for their return, she forgot to check her watch. As good as his word, Chance was soon back.

"Did you miss me?" he asked with a grin.

"Always." But at least this time she hadn't been a big bundle of nerves thanks to him giving her something else to ponder. Maybe that's what her father needed—something else to focus on besides her. He'd not dated since they had lost her mother. It was time for him to move on. Past time.

Maybe it was time for her to embrace life more as well. She'd taken a major step by coming to Honduras but not in her personal life. Working so hard to earn her independence, she'd put her love life on hold. Was it time for her to open up? Let someone in? Should that person be Chance? If she did, would he accept her?

"This is a good place to cross. The river is wide but not running fast."

Ellen picked up her pack. "At least I don't have to worry about saving your butt."

"Did I say thank you for that?"

She smiled. "I think you did but feel free to do so again."

"Thanks. Let's get moving."

She hurried to catch up with him. There was the old Chance. Focused.

The river was much wider than it had been where they had crossed before. The rocks were not nearly as large and were spaced so that one large step or jump could get her from one to another. There was a real possibility they could cross without getting wet.

"I want to lead this time." Ellen wasn't sure what had gotten into her when she said that.

Chance looked surprised. "Okay."

Ellen chose her path carefully, managing to get out into the middle of the river without any mishaps. There the water was moving faster and the gap between the rocks was wider. She hitched up her pack, preparing to jump. Pushing off hard, she jumped over the water and landed on her hands and knees on top of the next rock. Chance stepped up beside her. He took her forearm and helped her up.

"You're the most determined woman I know."

"Thanks." Ellen moved on across the river. When she reached the other side she waited for Chance to join her, which he soon did. "Come on. We need to get going." She headed down the path.

"So are you usurping my authority now?"

"I just thought I'd like to lead for a while. You know the saying: if you aren't the lead dog, the view never changes."

He released a bark of laughter. The birds reacted by screaming and flying away.

"Shush," she said.

Chance looked contrite then searched the area. His gaze came back to her. "No more smart remarks from you."

"You can't blame me for that. You were the one being loud."

They didn't walk long before the sound of civilization could be heard over the flow of water. Chance took the lead again, making his way into the greenery under a large tree. From their location they could see women doing laundry at the riverbank. There was an open field of high grass between the women and a group of huts sitting back against the jungle.

Chance put his mouth close to her ear. "We'll have to stay here until they leave. We might as well rest."

They slowly and as quietly as possible removed their packs. He leaned his back against the tree and she scooted up next to him. The women's chatter lulled her to sleep.

"Ow!" Ellen woke, slapping at her pants leg. She'd been bitten. Shaking out the material, she saw nothing.

Something was wrong. *Chance was gone.* Going up on her hands and knees, she searched the river area where the women had been. There was no one in sight.

Chance knew how she felt about being left alone. How could he disappear? Terror threatened to fill her chest but she pushed it down.

He would be back. He had to come back.

Off in the distance, downriver, clothes were hanging over a rope strung between two trees. There was a movement. One of the items disappeared from the line. *Chance.* She watched another piece of clothing being snatched away.

He would have to cross the field and come upriver again to get her. It would be safer if she met him. Quickly pulling on her pack and putting his bag across her chest, she carefully left her hiding place. With her body as low to the ground as possible she worked her way across the field. A dog barked. She crouched down. Her calf burned. She couldn't worry about that now.

Waiting for further noise and hearing none, she hurried to the jungle edge and along it to where she'd last seen Chance. There he was, pulling another item from the lie. She moved again to where she'd seen him duck out of the trees.

Chance's eyes went wide when he saw her. He handed her a couple of articles of clothing and nodded his head downriver. He didn't give her a chance to respond before he took his bag from her and quickly moved to the river and down the path. They walked at a rapid pace for a good while before he stepped off the trail.

Out of sight he turned to her. "You scared me to death, showing up like that."

"And you left me."

"I planned to be back before you woke."

She glared at him. "Don't do that to me again."

Chance studied her a second then said, "I won't. I promise."

She believed him. "I saw you and knew you'd have to double back for me so I decided to meet you."

"Smart girl."

"So what did you get us?" She rubbed her calf. It was still stinging. What had bitten her?

"Something for us to sleep on and a couple of clean shirts."

Ellen grinned. "I look forward to high-style living tonight. Shouldn't we get moving?"

"You're starting to sound like me." Chance smiled back and headed down the trail. Ellen had almost scared the life out of him when she'd shown up near the clothesline. He had really misjudged her when he'd first met her. Ellen had a backbone of iron.

When she'd announced that she was going to take the lead he couldn't help but be proud. If he had been in her place he would have been tired of following as well. The woman was full of surprises. His mother and ex-wife would have given up before they'd even got started. He wasn't used to having such a resilient woman in his life. *Life?* Could he really have her in his life? Would she stay with him?

He set a steady pace and Ellen kept up. A couple of times he checked behind him to see how she was doing. There was a determined look on her face, but occasionally her face was twisted as if she were in pain. Her feet must really be bothering her.

It was drawing close to evening and he had started to look for a place to stay for the night when the sounded of rushing water reached his ears.

"Is that a waterfall?" Ellen asked with enthusiasm.

"Sounds like one." If luck was with them they might have a good safe place to sleep and an opportunity for a fire. Even a bath.

They made a turn in the path and the water disappeared over the edge of a cliff.

He called back. "Are you up for a little climbing?"

Ellen shrugged. "Do I have a choice?"

"Not really. But if all goes well it'll be worth it."

"Lead on, then."

Over the next half an hour they made their way around and down to the pool of water at the bottom of the falls.

"It's amazing," Ellen said.

"It is. Honduras has incredible falls. I'd leave you here but I know you'd have none of that so come on and let's see if we can find a room for the night."

"Here?"

"Sure." Chance led the way around the pool toward the falls. He made a few maneuvers across rocks until they had worked their way behind it. There was the small cave he was looking for. It was large enough for them to remain dry and still have a small fire.

Pulling his bag off, he dropped the clothes on top. Speaking loudly, he worked at being heard over the roar of the water. "Your hotel room for the evening."

Ellen looked around. "It's wonderful."

"I need to look for something dry enough to burn before it gets too dark. Are you going to be okay here by yourself or do you want to come with me?"

"Aren't you worried about the smoke being seen?"

He smiled and pointed to the falls. "It'll blend in with the mist. We're safe. Hopefully we can have dry clothes."

She looked unsure a moment then straightened her shoulders. "No, I'll be fine here."

"I won't be long. Why don't you get that trash we have in our packs out to use as starter?"

It took Chance longer than he'd expected to find something in a tropical rain forest dry enough to burn. The entire time he was gone he worried about Ellen being frightened. He did manage to locate some dry leaves and small sticks. He and Ellen wouldn't have a bonfire but it would be something to dry clothes by.

With arms full, he made his way back to the river. He started to take his first step on the rocks when he saw her. Ellen stood naked beneath the falls. Her arms were raised as she held her hair out to let the water reach each strand. He'd never seen anything more breathtakingly beautiful or more uninhibited.

He should leave. Let her know he was there. But he couldn't.

Ellen turned, giving him a profile view of her delicious curves. His body hardened. Her breasts were high and her stomach flat. There was an arc to her behind that made his hands itch to hold her. He stood mesmerized by her splendor, unable to put a thought together beyond the acknowledgement of the desire building in him. Waiting and watching, he didn't want to disturb her or break the spell.

Ellen did it for him. She stepped out of the water. The gold of the evening sun caressed her skin as she walked to a nearby rock and gathered her clothes. She pulled on her shirt and pants and ducked behind the falls.

Chance remained where he was until he had control of his breathing. By the time he'd made it back to their hiding place some of his libido had eased but at the sight of Ellen it climbed again. He had to regain some perspective. It didn't help that Ellen's underwear lay in a small pile nearby.

The tension was thick between them. She wouldn't meet his gaze. Was she feeding off his emotion? Had she known that he'd been watching? It was as if the easiness between them over the last two days had disappeared and been replaced by the disquiet of heightened awareness of the weeks before. As alluring as Ellen had been as a water nymph minutes ago, he had to focus on them surviving. They needed to have a fire, eat and tend their feet. Those needs took precedence over his sexual cravings.

But those carnal needs pulled at him with each look he gave her.

He squatted and let the pile of brush fall from his arms. "Ellen, look in the side pocket of my bag and you'll find a round silver tube. Would you hand it to me?"

She did as he asked and included the trash as well.

He placed the paper under the brush and opened the watertight container, removing two matches.

"I should've known you'd have something up your sleeve to start a fire with."

"I keep them in case I have to go old school with sterilizing a needle. You just never know."

"Like this time."

He gave her a tight smile. "This was more than I planned for." Striking one match against the other, he quickly placed them on the paper. He slowly added some of the material he'd gathered until they had a small fire. "Bring your clothes over here and spread them out to dry. I wish this was going to be large enough for you to get your pants dry after a wash but I don't think they'll dry by morning. At least our underwear and shirts will be cleaner."

"Are you hungry?" she asked.

"Yes. I could eat."

"That was sort of a dumb question." Ellen picked up what little food they had and joined him beside the fire.

She gave him half of the food from the rag and ate the other. "That leaves us with one food bar."

"Hopefully we'll be in Saba by tomorrow night."

"As much as I've enjoyed this walk through the jungle, I have to admit I'm looking forward to seeing the resort again." She put the rag back in the backpack.

"Not New York? I would think after this you'd want to go home."

"No. Most of all I'd just like a good shower."

Chance looked at her. "I thought that's what you were having a few minutes ago." Even in the glow of the fire he could see her blush.

"You weren't supposed to see me."

He stood. "How was it?"

"Wonderful."

"If you'll keep the fire going I think I'll give the falls a try as well."

Ellen watched Chance leave. She wasn't sure why she had suddenly turned bashful around him. It was as if they had been fighting for their lives every hour of the last two days and she now felt safe enough to think of living. The intimate space they would share for the night only added to that awareness. She still tingled all over with the knowledge he had watched her bathe. For how long?

The waterfall had looked so inviting. She hadn't felt nastier in her entire life. Dirt mixed with sweat, her clothes sticking to her, pants less black than tan. Her hair had been a mass of tangles with bits of leaf and twigs. No one at home would have recognized her. The rush of the water had called to her. She had planned it to be a quick bath but she'd become caught up in the heavenly feeling of the water flowing over her and had stayed longer than she'd intended.

Ellen looked at the falls. She couldn't see Chance

through the rush of water but she could picture him beneath it as water washed over his shoulders and ran down his chest. What if they didn't make it home the next day? Were caught? Never had a chance to be together?

What would it be like to really spend a night in his arms? Life was too short not to have that pleasure.

She spread the blanket out near the fire and stored their packs. Her leg let her know it was there as she moved. Sitting down, she pulled her pants leg up and twisted so she could see the back of her calf. There was a red welt just above where the top of her boot came. She had been bitten. It was tender and warm. There wasn't much she could do about it now. She'd check it again in the morning.

Pulling Chance's pack to her, she found the ointment and gave her feet some much-needed attention. Her blisters now had blisters. She dreaded putting her boots on in the morning. At least her socks had been rinsed, which would help cut down on infection. She would lose one of her big toenails, if not both.

Chance joined her. His hair was wet. He'd pushed it away from his forehead. A lock of it hadn't stayed in place. Bare-chested and with his pants low on his hips, he strolled toward her. The fire reflected off his still-damp skin. Every nerve in her body was alert to him.

He laid his clothing beside hers. There was something oddly intimate about their undergarments drying next to each other.

"You need to get some sleep. We have another day of walking ahead of us." He put another piece of brush on the fire.

He continued to stand as if he wasn't going to join her on the blanket. "You aren't going to sleep?"

"I think I'll sit up for a while."

"Then I'll keep you company unless you've had enough of it."

"I don't think that's possible." A stricken look covered his features as if he'd said something he hadn't meant to.

"We haven't had that talk yet," she said just loud enough that she could be heard over the falls.

"Ellen, I don't think—"

"You're right. I don't want to talk." She stood. "I've spent the last two days worrying about dying."

"Ellen..."

She stepped around the fire. "There might not be another day, another time and I want to celebrate being alive. With you." Placing her hands on his shoulders, she went up on her toes and kissed him.

Chance grabbed her around the waist. Pulling her against his chest, he brought her feet off the ground. His mouth devoured hers as if he was hungry and a banquet was being served.

CHAPTER SEVEN

HOW LIKE ELLEN to take the initiative. Chance wasn't going to turn her away again. The gentleman in him he'd left in that hovel days before. He was going to accept what was offered. All of Ellen.

He would inhale her, touch her, have her. Totally take what he'd desired for weeks.

His body was tense with anticipation. With one hot kiss his manhood stood ready. He craved everything about her.

With her still in his arms he walked around the fire to the blanket. She wrapped her arms around his neck as they went. Cupping the back of his head, she held his mouth to hers. Her tongue caressed, twirled and mated with his, mimicking the very things he wanted to do to her.

Chance hadn't planned this. But he wanted it. Needed her.

She was right. They had spent the last few days fighting for their lives. He didn't want to battle himself or her about the attraction between them. Now it was time to feel her against him for the pleasure of her, not for the need to survive. Chance eased her down his body and brought his hands up under her shirt tracing the lines of her body. Stepping away, he pulled her shirt over her head and dropped it to the stone floor.

She was stunning, standing before him. The flickering firelight touched her in places he had every intention of savoring. He cupped one of her breasts. Slowly, he pulled his hand away, caressing the breast from beneath. Ellen shivered, adding to his delight. He reveled in her soft sound of pleasure.

The pads of her fingers drifted over his chest then downward to the edge of his pants and around to his side. She slipped a finger beneath his waistband and moved it across his skin.

His manhood tightened. Strained against the front of his pants.

She grabbed a handful of material and pulled him to her.

Chance took her mouth again. This time she brought a leg up his, circling it with hers. He broke the kiss and looked into her eyes. "I desperately want you but I can't make any promises."

"Tonight isn't about promises. It's about being alive. Enjoying life."

She hadn't said it but he knew her too well not to know she cared deeply for people and that meant she didn't take relationships lightly. Should he let this continue? For his sake? Hers?

A hint of a smile came to Ellen's lips. "Remember what I said that day when I was polishing the girl's nails? A moment of pleasure is better than none. If something happens to you, I'd always regret not having you like this."

That brick wall Chance had built around his heart had just taken a battering. He couldn't let her get hurt. "This isn't some storybook adventure that's going to end in a happily-ever-after."

"Have I ever said that's what I want?"

She hadn't, and for some reason it stung that she didn't expect it.

Her hands ran up his ribs and down his arms. "What I'm saying is that I want you. I know you want me. I feel it." She flexed forward. "There might not be another time. We may not get out of this. I don't want any regrets. Not being with you would be a great regret."

Chance knew about regrets and disappointment. He'd experienced both a number of times in his life. With his mother. His sister. His ex-wife. Ellen wouldn't be one of those. He would see to that right now.

Cupping her face with his hands, he gave her a gentle kiss. "You deserve a big comfortable bed and someplace clean."

"I don't care as long as you are there."

Bam. There went another chip in the wall.

Pulling her against him, Chance savored the feel of her bare breasts against his chest. His mouth found hers again then moved over her cheek to kiss the hollow behind her ear. She tilted her head as if asking for more.

He found her waistband and unfastened the button. Deliberately, he pulled the zipper down. Her pants fell to her feet and she pushed them away. His mouth left her ear to travel over the ridge of her shoulder and down to the tip of one breast.

His mouth took it, sucked. Running his tongue around the nipple, he teased.

A soft, sensual sigh filled the air as Ellen combed her fingers through his hair.

Chance pulled away and blew over the damp mound he was giving attention to. Ellen's moan turned to a groan.

His length twitched. How much longer could he stand not having her? What would she sound like when she found release?

Cupping the other breast, he took it into his mouth, giving it the same attention as he'd lavished on the first. She held his head, encouraging him. Chance's mouth left her breast to kiss his way up her neck and capture her lips. The meeting of mouths was wild and hot.

Her hands went to his pants and released them, pushing them over his hips to the ground. She didn't hesitate before she wrapped her hand around his staff and gently stroked. If she kept that up he would combust before they made it to the blanket.

Chance moved back and she released him. "I'll lose control if you touch me."

"I don't care." Her voice was husky, which did nothing to ease his need.

"But I do. You deserve more." He kissed her deeply. One of his hands followed the curve of her shoulder, skimmed her breast to brush the line of her hip. The palm of his hand skimmed over her stomach before his fingers teased the curls between her legs.

She tensed in his arms.

He slid a finger between her folds and pulled away.

Ellen shook, making a delicious sound of protest.

Chance cupped her center then slowly pulled a finger between her folds. Her stance widened as her tongue entered his mouth. She clung to his shoulders. Using one finger, he went deeper, finding the wet, hot opening of her desire. He dipped the tip of his finger inside. Ellen hissed close to his ear. Bringing her leg up around his, she offered him clear passage. He took it, pushing his finger completely into her. She bucked, going up on her toes.

He removed his finger and pushed into her again. Her hips flexed against him. She clawed at his back. Retreating, he thrust again. This time Ellen pushed down on his hand. Pulling his finger away, he entered her again. Her head fell back. Her hair was wild around her shoulders as she cried her pleasure and withered against him.

It took all Chance had within him not to throw Ellen to the ground and hammer into her.

Instead he held her, watching the soft look settle over her face as she eased to earth once more. The experience was something he'd never had with a woman before. It left a feeling of satisfaction he wasn't familiar with but desperately wanted again.

Was that another brick being knock away?

Ellen relaxed against him. He removed his finger and grasped her waist. Their gazes met. Hers was dewy. She gave him the tiny smile of a woman who'd found something special. He stood on top of the world because he was the one who'd given it to her.

That was an awesome responsibility. Did he want to carry that? Could he take that gamble?

Ellen placed a hand in one of his, went down on the blanket and pulled him to her.

Chance didn't resist. He couldn't.

"You deserve some attention." Her voice was deeper and even sexier than before.

"It's not necessary."

There was a look of concern in her eyes for a second then her lips turned upward. "Oh, but I think it is."

Ellen wanted to give Chance some of the pleasure he'd given her. She wasn't inexperienced but nothing she had felt before compared to what Chance's touch had done to her.

When he'd said it wasn't necessary she'd feared he was running away again. She wasn't going to let that happen.

Lying on her side, she faced him. His masculinity was almost more than she could comprehend. Holding his gaze, she reached out and placed her hand on the pectoral muscles of his chest then ran her index finger over his skin. Slowly she traced his ribs, dipping and rising as she moved downward.

She glanced up to see that Chance's pupils had dilated. They burned with desire. Her actions were having the effect she desired. Circling his belly button, she enjoyed the inhalation of his breath as she watched his skin react to her touch. It was exciting to see this strong, masterful man respond to her. Her hand followed a line of hair downward until she reached the head of his manhood. She ran the tip of her finger over him and watched the length twitch.

Chance growled and pulled her hand away.

Grinning, Ellen shifted so that she could push his shoulders to the blanket. That done, she straddled him. She kissed his jaw and moved down to the valley of his neck and onto his chest. As she went one of Chance's hands glided over her hip. When her tongue slid across his breastbone, he cupped a butt cheek and gently squeezed.

She rose above him. Looking into his eyes, Ellen slowly came down to kiss him. It was a kiss of not only passion but of heartfelt longing and caring.

Chance took control and rolled her to her back. One of his legs came to rest over hers. "I can't last much longer. I promise you slow next time."

Her heart swelled. He thought there would be a next time.

Ellen lifted her hips, pushing her center against his leg. She throbbed for him. Blood rushed in her ears. She needed him as well.

Chance settled between her legs, his manhood coming to rest at her entrance. He supported himself on his elbows as he looked down at her.

A stricken look crossed his face. "We have no protection."

Ellen's hands found his hips and pulled him to her as

she lifted upward. "Don't worry. I have it taken care of." She reached up and kissed him with everything in her. She refused to let him leave her again.

Chance slipped into her until she held all of him. Ellen gripped his forearms and wrapped her legs around his waist, bringing him closer. He pulled back and pushed forward then did it again. Each time tension coiled tighter in her. She wiggled, begging to have more. Chance gifted her with a hard thrust.

Ellen squeezed her legs tighter around him, bowed her back as he pressed into her. Squeezing her eyes shut, she reached, searched and grabbed for what she needed. Finding the pinnacle, she came apart. She remained rigid, taking all Chance had to offer, until she started the blissful float downward.

Her legs fell away from his hips. Before she could think straight again Chance drove into her. Slowly at first, then faster he stoked. Her hands tightened around his neck. He grasped her hips and held her firmly against him. His mouth took hers and whatever else he wanted. Heat flared in her. She grasped his shoulders. It couldn't be happening again. Chance gained speed. Her scream of pleasure mixed with his groan of release as he sent her to the stars once more.

Chance held Ellen close as they lay on the too-small blanket. Her head lay against his shoulder and her arm rested across his chest with her hand buried under his hair. One of her legs wrapped around his and her foot was cupped in the arch of his.

She fit like she belonged. Perfectly. What would it be like to have her like this all the time?

He'd never been more satisfied in his life. She was everything he'd never thought to have in a woman. Beauty, intelligence, strength, passion, perseverance and most of all an easy smile. He shouldn't think like that but having Ellen in his arms made him want to dream again. She'd brought that back to his life.

Her hand moved over his shoulder and teased his earlobe.

He looked at her. "Hey, there. I thought you were asleep."

"Mmm… Just resting." She stretched against him, running her fingers across his belly.

"You keep that up and I'll have to retaliate."

"I don't have a problem with that." She kissed his neck. "Didn't you promise me slow next time?"

Chance kissed the top of her head as his hand caressed the under-curve of one of her breasts. "I can go slow. But the question is can you stand it?"

Ellen's hand drifted to his hip. "As long as you can."

He took the challenge and they both won.

They were still basking in a cloud of satisfaction while in each other's arms when Ellen said, "Tell me about your childhood."

Chance couldn't help but flinch. Why did Ellen want to know about that? He'd rather talk about anything else but that and his ex-wife. She'd already heard that sordid story.

"I was a baby, then a child and now a man. Pretty typical stuff."

She gave him a playful swat on the chest. "I know well that you are a man. But what I want to know about is Chance the little boy."

Ellen wasn't going to back off from this. That wasn't who she was. He might as well tell her and then she'd quit asking. "I was raised in upstate New York. My father was a world-famous surgeon even when I was a young boy. He traveled and spoke a lot. We had everything money could buy but he was never around. My mother adored him." Chance had worshiped his mother. "But my father was so wrapped up in his life that he barely saw her. He liked the jet-setting, being the big shot, and he like the women that went with that recognition. I'm not sure why they ever married."

The same question had occurred to him when Alissa had left him. Had he, like his father, been so wrapped up in his work that he hadn't been taking care of what he'd needed to do at home? Had it been fair to ask a woman to live his lifestyle? The question still nagged at him.

He looked at Ellen. Her golden hair was spread out over his chest and shoulder. Her fingers ran along the center of his chest as if she couldn't get enough of him.

"How sad. Your mother must have been so lonely."

"She was."

"What happened?"

His chest tightened. "How did you know something happened?"

"By the tone of your voice."

Had he become that transparent? Or was she just that in tune with him? He wasn't sure which idea disturbed him more. "She left. Later I was told she joined a commune-type place. As far as I know, she's still there. I went to see her once when I was in college but she said she didn't want to see me. I never tried again."

Ellen's arm went to his waist and she gave him a tight hug. "Oh, Chance, I'm so sorry."

She'd lost her mother as well. If anyone could empathize it was her. "You understand too well, don't you?"

Her head nodded against him. "Mothers are important." She didn't say anything for a few minutes. Her voice wobbled as she said, "I watched my mother die."

Even during this ordeal she'd never sounded so close to tears. They shared a huge loss but hers had been far more traumatizing. He pulled her close. If only he could take her pain away. "Sweetheart, I'm so sorry."

Chance understood her agony. Knew the need of a child for comfort that only a mother could give. Or the smell of perfume that was hers alone. A whisper of a kiss on the cheek as she went by or that safe feeling when being tucked in at night.

Yet despite their similarities in background, Ellen saw the world as a sparkling place while he saw it as tarnished. She seemed to bubble even in the situation they were in now. He wanted that in his life.

Moisture touched his skin. Strong, resilient Ellen was crying for two children who had lost their mothers. Chance's chest tightened. His father not caring was painful but his mother's defection was devastating. At least Ellen hadn't felt unloved. He squeezed her close as she cried. "I'm sorry about your mother too."

Minutes later she composed herself again then said, "Who would have thought we'd share something so awful?"

He kissed the top of her head. "I, for one, would prefer to remember something else we've shared."

Ellen moved to look up at him with eyes that were still misty. "Why, Dr. Freeman, I believe there might be a romantic under all that gruff and bluster."

He smiled. "Don't get that rumor started."

At least they had moved past that emotional moment but they continued to hold each for some time.

Finally Ellen asked, "Will you tell me the rest of the story now? Did your father come home then?"

"Yeah, just long enough to put me and my sister into boarding schools."

"You have a sister?"

"I do."

Ellen grabbed a shirt and pulled it on. "But you've never said anything about her."

He shrugged. "I don't really know her."

"How can you not know your sister?"

"Pretty easy when I only saw her once a year at Christmas."

"What? That's horrible."

"Maybe so, but that's the way it was."

"Still is, I gather." Ellen sounded as if she was accusing him of doing something appalling in a court of law.

He sat up and faced her. "We're just in two different worlds. She has her life and I have mine."

"So you didn't even have each other to lean on when your mother left. No wonder you have issues with women. Pushed me away," she murmured.

Chance stiffened. "Don't start analyzing me."

"It was more of an observation."

He didn't like that much better. Had Ellen seen something about him that not even he was aware of?

"Where's your father?"

"He died a couple of years ago."

"I don't know what I would have done without my father. He's been there for me all the way."

"That must be nice."

"It is, most of the time."

Chance was relieved they had moved past the subject of him. "Most of the time?"

"I told you, he tends to watch over me too much."

"I can understand a father wanting to protect you."

She chuckled. "I guess you can. You act like him sometimes."

"Is that so bad?"

"What, that you act like him? Or that he is overprotective?"

"The overprotective part." He studied her. Her hands were clasped in her lap in a ball.

"It is when you want to do more than work on the upper

east side and in a hospital for women having their faces and breasts done."

He ran his palm lightly over one of her nipples. "Which you need neither of."

Ellen caught his hand and held it. "Thank you. But I wanted to work where people needed me. Where others weren't as willing to go."

"So what made you want to do that?"

"I don't know really. I guess it was because of what my doctors and nurses meant to me."

She waited as if she were in deep thought. He knew her well enough to know she would tell all if he just had the patience to wait.

"I still stay in touch with them."

"Who?"

"My doctor and nurses. I was in the car with my mother. I was in the hospital for weeks afterwards."

"That's why you balked the first day."

"Yeah. I've not done much emergency care and it takes me a second but I come around."

"And you did. And did great."

"Thanks. But that's not what you thought then. I saw it in your eyes."

"Guilty. But tell me about your father."

"He was devastated after my mother's death. He was at the hospital with me but he was so broken he wasn't much good around me. It was the doctors and nurses who looked after me. Brought me fast food. Talked and played with a scared little girl. I decided then that I wanted to be like them.

"It took a while but my father found his way out of his grief to see me again and then all he could think about was not losing me. I understand that but it can be stifling. When I went to work at an inner-city clinic he pitched a fit and hired a bodyguard to watch over me. Let's just say there was a large discussion over that. I didn't tell him until the night before I left to come down here that I was coming. Even then I didn't tell him where. I'm sure by now he knows about the resort."

Chance was sure her father didn't know the exact spot they were in now or they would have been rescued. If he ever met her father Chance was sure there would be hell to pay. A father who worried over his daughter that deeply wouldn't like her running for her life in the jungle or sleeping with the man who was responsible for the situation. It was just as well this thing between he and Ellen would end when she left Honduras. Why did the thought gnaw at him so much?

"At least your father cares. Mine hardly knew I was alive."

"That shouldn't have happened to you. I'm surprised you became a doctor like him."

"I was good at science and math. Medicine was—is—in my DNA. But I wanted to be a very different type of person from my father. From the beginning I wanted to help the less privileged."

"You are different. I can't see you not watching over the people you love and showing you care. Look what you're doing for the people of this country."

Her conviction had Chance wanting to believe her. He gave her a kiss that had nothing to do with wanting her sexually and everything to do with appreciating her large heart and loyalty. He needed both in his life.

Chance stood. "Enough talking or you'll have me telling stories of how I misbehaved in school."

"You were a troublemaker?"

"Only until the headmaster sat me down and said a few pointed words that made me think." He reached out his hand. "How about a moonlight trip to the falls?"

"Aren't you afraid we might be seen?"

"We won't stay long. I just keep thinking about you bathing and how much I wished I'd joined you."

"With an invitation like that, how can I refuse?" She took his hand.

Ellen couldn't remember ever being this uninhibited with a man before. She let Chance remove the shirt she'd pulled on and then held his hand as they carefully stepped over the rocks and into the falls under the full moon.

The ache in her leg had been forgotten as Chance had turned her mind toward what he'd been doing to her body. Then her entire attention had been focused on what he'd been saying. She was surprised by how open he'd been that she'd hung on each of his words.

Now there was an aching throb in her calf but as Chance pulled her under the falls it was eclipsed by the touch of his hands running over her waist and hips. She threw her head back and let the water wash through her hair as he kissed her shoulder and cupped her breasts.

There was something wanton, liberating, almost wicked about standing out in the middle of the world with no clothes on as a man loved her body. A tingle in her center grew to a pounding as blood flowed hot within her. She was a siren calling to her mate.

Her hands skimmed over Chance's wet arms and down his back as he kissed the outside of one breast. As he stood there she pushed his hair away from his face. His manhood, thick and tall, found the V of her legs as his mouth came to hers. His hands cupped her butt and lifted. She circled his hips with her legs. Chance shoved once and completely entered her. She held tightly to his shoulders. He eased away and pushed forward. She shuttered. He plunged deeper and joined her in the pleasure.

Chance released her, letting her slid down his wet body. He kissed her deeply then led her out of the falls and over the rocks. "As much as I'm enjoying your body, we need to get some sleep. We still have a day of walking tomorrow. We aren't out of danger yet."

"Boy, you have a way of putting a damper on the afterglow."

He gave her a quick kiss as they returned to their hiding place. "I'll do better next time but I want us to make it to the next time." Picking up a few sticks, he put them on the fire, which had turned to coals. "We need to dry off and get some sleep. As much as I hate to say this, we should sleep in our clothes in case we need to make a quick getaway."

Ellen picked up her underwear and began putting them on. "Is that your way of telling me you've seen all of my body you want to?"

Chance stepped to her and tipped her chin up with a finger. "I could never get enough of looking at your body."

Warmth went through her, settling in her heart. She wanted this moment, this feeling between them, always.

CHAPTER EIGHT

CHANCE WOKE. HE was hot. Too hot. On the side where Ellen rested. She was running a fever.

She groaned and sat up. Her eyes were red and face flushed. Little beads of sweat lined her upper lip.

Chance touched her cheek and confirmed what he already knew. This wasn't good. They already had a day's worth of travel ahead but with her sick it would slow them down.

"I don't feel well."

"I'm not surprised. You're running a pretty high fever. I'll check it in a minute. Do you hurt somewhere?" If they were lucky it was an intestinal problem from the food or lack of it.

"My leg."

He searched her face. "Your leg?"

"Something bit me yesterday when you were stealing clothes."

"Why didn't you say something?" She should have told him, especially after the number of bite cases they'd seen at the clinic. She knew better than to let something like that wait. Panic started to clench his gut.

"Show me."

"Can I have a drink of water first?" She lay back on the blanket.

Ellen was already too weak to sit up for any length of time. Chance picked up a bottle. Going down on one knee, he put an arm around her shoulders and supported her. Slowly she drank.

"Can I sleep a little longer?"

"Sure, sweetheart. Sleep while I look at your leg. Which one is it?"

Ellen stretched out her right leg. "Calf."

Chance pushed up the leg of her pants to reveal a large angry place that covered her calf from the back of her knee to her ankle. In the center there was a boil surrounded by deep purple. His heart constricted. Ellen should be in a hospital. Even if he lanced it the risk of infection was too great and she truly couldn't walk then.

"I wish you had said something." He wanted to shake her and hug her at the same time. They had little water, no food, and now Ellen was seriously sick. His concern for them getting out of this mess today had escalated a hundred percent.

"I was going to, but I was busy doing other things last night." There was humor in her voice.

"We were both thinking of other things last night."

Now he carried that burden of guilt. He should have stayed focused on their problem; instead he had been satisfying his need for her. That was another issue. He wasn't satisfied. Not by a long shot. But he wouldn't be misdirected by his desire again. It could mean Ellen's life and he couldn't abide anything more happening to her. He had to get them out of this new situation and Ellen safely home.

She started to rise.

"Stay put. I'm going to give you a quick exam. Then we'll need to get moving." Chance pulled his bag closer and removed his stethoscope then the thermometer. "Let's see how high your fever is while I'm giving you a good listen."

Her grin was weak as she said, "I like the good things you give me."

How like Ellen to speak frankly, even about a night of passion. He kissed her forehead. "I enjoyed it too. Now stop distracting me and let me see how you're doing."

"I'm distracting you?"

"Sweetheart, you've been distracting me for weeks." Chance placed the stethoscope on her chest. Her heartbeat was steady, which was encouraging. He checked her pulse and blood pressure. They were up a little bit. Removing the thermometer, he wasn't pleased. He searched his med bag and found a bottle of aspirin. It wouldn't do much for the fever but it was better than nothing.

"Do you think you're up for some walking?" He was sure she wasn't but they really had no choice but to get moving. She wouldn't last another day in the heat and rain with that leg.

"Sure."

He didn't expect her to say anything different.

"Could I have that half of a bar now instead of later?"

"That's a great idea. We'll share it for breakfast. I also want you to take a couple of aspirin for me." He handed her the bar, medicine and set a bottle of water down beside her.

They ate in silence.

Done with her bar, Ellen said, "I'm sorry, but I'm going to need your help with my boot."

Chance assisted her with getting the boot on her foot but could only lace it up loosely around her calf. He was afraid that before the day was over she would be in real pain.

When they were done, he packed the bags except for

the rag the boy had placed the food in. He pulled the strap of his bag over his chest and shrugged into the backpack.

"What're you doing?" Ellen stood beside him. "I'll carry the backpack. That's my job."

"Today you get a day off. Come on, let's get going."

They headed out from behind the falls. Chance stopped a few times to make sure no one else was around.

When they came to the pool, he dipped the rag into the water, wetting it thoroughly, then wrung it out. "Ellen, come here." She stepped closer to him. He wrapped the rag around her head. "This'll help keep you cooler."

Her gaze found his. "Thank you. You're a good person, Chance Freeman."

Coming from her, the simple compliment sounded like he was receiving a great honor in front of thousands. He brushed her lips with his. "You're quite a woman yourself, Ellen Cox."

Chance set a slower pace than he had the days before but even then Ellen was lagging behind. What had at first been a slow walk had now turned into one that included a limp. They stopped often to rest but that didn't seem to give her any more energy. With each stop he wet the rag and retied it across her forehead.

Her fever eased at one point but by midmorning it had returned with a vengeance. He was going to have to find another way to get them to Saba sooner rather than later. Ellen couldn't continue the way she was going. During one of their rests he'd looked at her leg. It was more inflamed than before. Walking hadn't helped.

It hurt him to see her in pain. Yet she still didn't complain.

"Chance, I'm sorry I got us into this and now I'm holding us up."

"For starters, you didn't get us into this. I agreed to see the boy's father. I knew the risks. That's all on me. As for your leg, yes, you should have told me sooner but there isn't much more we could have done. You didn't get bitten on purpose. So enough of that kind of talk."

"My, you are being all noble. But, then, that's who you are."

She made the statement sound as if she knew few people who were noble and admired him for it. He liked having Ellen think he was someone special.

By noon, he had to walk beside her while she leaned on him in order for her to move. Each time her injured leg touched the ground she winced. They had stopped again to rest when Chance said, "I'm going to have to carry you."

Thankfully the land had flattened out. The river was wider and slower, letting him know that were getting close to the coast.

Ellen shook her head. "How long would you last, doing that in this heat? Leave me and go for help."

"What?" She'd been terrified when he been gone for only minutes. He couldn't leave her with a dangerously high fever out in the jungle alone. "No way. We're in this together."

"I could never forgive myself if something happened to you because of me."

Chance cupped her face. "I think that's my line. Now, let's not talk about it any more. We're going to try you riding on my back for a while."

"Okay, but you let me have the packs."

He removed them and helped her on with them.

"Okay, you ready?" He squatted so she could reach around his neck.

She did so. Her heat seeped through his shirt. He wrapped his arms under her thighs and lifted her on his back as he stood. Chance started down the path. It wasn't an easy trek but it was far better than seeing Ellen's misery. They made it further than Chance had thought they would before he had to rest. Ellen could hardly keep her eyes open she was so consumed by fever. He had to find help soon or she would be in real danger of having lasting side effects.

"It's time to go again." She offered little help getting on his back. The fever was taking her energy.

Again Chance trudged down the path. There wasn't a dry stitch of clothes on either one of them. Sweat poured from where their bodies met. He leaned forward so that Ellen rested on his back more than held on. She'd long ago become heavier and her arms more relaxed. Had she passed out?

The river now stretched out more like a placid lake. High grass grew on each side of the path. The jungle was far off to the sides, affording them little protection. The only plan Chance had for them finding cover was to go into the grass and lie down, hoping they weren't seen. He'd reached the point that he needed someone to see them. It would be an opportunity to get help for Ellen.

With an amount of relief he hadn't known it was possible to feel, he heard the sounds of life carried over the water. There must be a village close by. He took Ellen to a spot far enough off the path that he believed she would be safe. He then eased her from his back and to the ground. There was no argument. She was unconscious. At least she wasn't feeling any pain.

He removed the packs and placed his under her head. Checking her pulse, he was glad to find that it was strong but she burned with fever. He pulled a bottle out and poured a few drops of water into her mouth. Watching her swallow, he gave her some more. He then drank a mouthful, leaving the bottle beside her in case she woke.

Kissing her on the forehead, he headed back to the path at almost a run. He hated leaving Ellen by herself but at least she was unaware he was doing so. That way she wouldn't fear being left alone.

When he reached the river he continued his pace along the path. After a couple of turns he came to a village of stilted homes built out over the water. These were much nicer dwellings constructed of finer material than those he had seen before. Still small, they appeared as if they might have more than one room.

Boats were tied below a number of them. Maybe he could find someone to take him and Ellen downriver. He continued running. A couple of children played in a bare spot at the bottom of a ladder to one of the huts. They chattered when they saw him and a woman stepped out onto the porch. Raising a hand to her forehead as if blocking the sun, she watched him approach.

Chance slowed his pace to a jog. He didn't want to scare away any aid he might find. "I need help," he called in Spanish. "A woman is sick."

A couple of other villagers exited their huts.

"I'm a doctor. I need to borrow a boat."

A young man joined the children as if in protective mode.

Chance stopped before he got too close to the first hut. "I have a sick woman with me. We need to get to Saba. I can pay for the boat. I'm Dr. Chance Freeman. I work with the Traveling Clinic out of La Ceiba."

Hopefully they had heard of the clinic. Maybe someone they knew had come to it.

The young man spoke up. "I know of it."

"Can you help me?" There was desperation in every word. Chance would get down on his knees and beg if he had to. All his fear was for Ellen. Her life. Had she woken? Found herself alone? He'd promised not to leave her again, yet he had. "Will you take me downriver to Saba?"

The young man looked around at the women then back at Chance. "I have no boat."

"What about these?" Chance waved his hand in the direction of the boats under the huts.

"Not mine."

The woman standing above them said, "Take my husband's. But you better return it."

"Come," the young man said, and headed toward the boat under the hut.

He didn't have to ask Chance twice. The man untied the boat and held it. The craft reminded Chance of a canoe with a flat bottom. There were no benches to sit on so he took a seat on the planks. The vessel seemed water-worthy enough but at this point it didn't matter. He needed to get back to Ellen. The man pushed away from shore, using a long-handled narrow paddle.

"We must go upstream, two bends in the path." Chance pointed in the direction he wanted them to go.

The man nodded and pushed against the bottom of the shallow riverbed, turning the boat so that Chance sat in the front. They headed upstream. Keeping the boat close to the shore, the man maneuvered them toward Ellen's hiding place. Even with the regular flap-flap of the water against the hull, they weren't moving fast enough for Chance. Worry circled like a wild animal in him.

"Here." Chance pointed to the shore. "Stop here."

The man directed the boat to land and it had hardly hit when Chance stepped out. He didn't wait on the man before he found the path along the river and backtracked to where Ellen waited. Running through the grass, he found her where he had left her. She looked as if she hadn't moved.

He went down beside her and lifted her head to his thigh. "Sweetheart. Wake up."

"You left me."

Great. If he didn't already feel horrible.

"I did but I'm back now. I found a boat and someone to take us to Saba."

"Good. I'm looking forward to sleeping in a bed with you."

"That sounds wonderful to me too but right now we need to get you to a hospital."

The young man arrived and looked down on them with curiosity.

Chance scooped Ellen into his arms. Her head rested against his chest. Even in the tropical weather he could tell her fever was still running high. "Please get the packs," he said to the man. Chance didn't wait to see if he did as he had asked. His concern was for getting Ellen to medical care as soon as possible, even if he had to steal the boat.

It wasn't an issue. The man passed him and Ellen on the path and was waiting at the boat when they arrived. Chance laid Ellen in the bottom then climbed in and sat behind her, situating her head against his thigh.

She sighed and closed her eyes. The man pushed the boat out into the river. Soon they were in the main channel.

"How long to Saba?" Chance asked over his shoulder.

"Dark. Maybe sooner."

Chance wasn't pleased with the answer. That was three or four hours away. He brushed Ellen's hair back from her forehead. She mumbled something unintelligible. Her soft skin was damaged from the sun, her lips parched and swollen. She was dehydrated. The list could go on and on.

Her hand found his and held it against her cheek. "I'll be fine."

Chance kissed the top of her head. "Sure you will." He wouldn't allow himself to think otherwise.

What in her made her so tough? It had to have been when she had been trapped in the wreck with her mother.

She'd known pain on a physical and emotional level that most people never experienced. How long had they waited for help? What had the pain been like as she'd healed? For her, this bug bite wasn't unendurable. She'd learned early in life what she could withstand.

He'd been playing her protector when Ellen was already a survivor.

Chance looked down into her beautiful face. She had the strength that it took to live and work here. Ellen didn't give up, she persevered. She wasn't a quitter. When she made a commitment it was forever. Could he open his heart enough to accept that?

If Ellen died Chance was afraid he would too. Despite what he had already lost in the world, his family, his wife, Ellen would be the greatest loss. When had she cracked through that wall and stepped into his heart? Had it been when she'd pulled out that hot pink nail polish, or stood up to him about his feelings for her, or her determination to care for a patient? Whenever it had been, she'd done it. He'd fallen for her.

The knowledge didn't make him feel better. He looked down at Ellen again. She just couldn't die now that he'd found someone who he knew with all his heart would stand by him the rest of his life.

Over the next few hours he bathed her head, neck and chest with the wet cloth, hoping he could keep the fever at bay. He did manage to get some water down her. But she needed so much care that he didn't have available. Even unconscious most of the time, she clutched his hand.

The sun was low in the sky when the man said, "Saba."

Relief washed through Chance. They were finally back in civilization.

"Help's not far away, sweetheart." He brushed a damp strand of hair away from Ellen's face. "We'll have you in a hospital soon."

Ahead Chance saw a high, modern bridge spanning the river. He'd heard of it but had never seen it. It was a major thoroughfare over the river and to the coast. And an answer to his prayers.

"I stop," the young man said as he pulled over to a pier. "Water too low past here."

Chance stepped out of the boat with Ellen in his arms and with the help of the man. "Thank you. I hope I'm able to repay you one day," Chance said, then hurried toward land.

He searched the area. Now he had to find a phone to call for help or someone to take them to the hospital. Determination and anxiety mixed, becoming a lump in his chest.

Chance hurried up a wide path with low green vegetation on each side toward houses. The path turned into a hard-packed dirt road wide enough for two cars. The houses lining the road were square and made of cinder block and plaster with only man-sized alleys between them. Chairs sat outside many of them.

Wasn't someone around?

The boy of about ten played in the street up ahead. "Help. Hospital."

Eyes going wide, the boy looked at him then ran into a nearby house.

He had to look like someone straight out of the child's bad dreams. With three days of growth on his face, his clothes dirty and smelly, and holding a woman burning with fever in his arms, he must look horrible.

A heavy woman appeared in the door of the house the child had run into.

Hope swelled. "Please help me. I have a sick woman. I need a phone or a way to the hospital."

"No phone. The boy will take you to someone who can help."

The boy was already headed up the street. Chance lifted Ellen more securely against his chest and followed. They walked a block and the boy ran up to a man talking to a group of other men. He pulled on the man's arm. The boy pointed to them. The man stepped away from the group and came toward Chance.

"I need a hospital. Do you have a phone? A car?"

"Car. Come this way." The man directed Chance toward a rusty and dented old sedan. Chance had never been so glad to see anything in his life. Opening the back door, the man then moved away so that Chance could place Ellen inside.

She opened her eyes for a second. "Where are we?"

"In Saba and on our way to the hospital, sweetheart."

"I like sweetheart."

Chance couldn't help but smile. "Good. I like calling you that."

As ill and in pain as Ellen must be, she still had a positive attitude. She'd told him she was tougher than she looked and she was right. Her life hadn't always been easy but she'd managed to find humor and wonder in it.

Convinced by his first impression and his past prejudice that she was weak and needy, he'd learned through this ordeal she was actually the stronger one of the two of them. He'd not been pushing her away for her good but his. What if he pursued a relationship and she rejected him? Would he survive the loss? Would he regret it more if he didn't try?

"No hospital close by," the man said.

Chance was afraid of that. "Where?"

"San Pedro Sula." The man glanced at Ellen. "I take there."

That hope started to build again. Chance had never been there before but that didn't matter. Ellen needed care.

They bounced over rocks and through ditches as the

car rattled up the unpaved street. The going was excruciatingly slow for Chance but they were moving toward help for Ellen. He was sitting in the back, with her head resting in his lap. Checking her vitals for the second time since they had left the boat, he was terrified by what he found. Her heart rate was becoming irregular. Her blood pressure was very high as well as her fever.

He looked up when the tires of the car hit pavement and his teeth quit knocking together. The car picked up speed and they were soon rolling over the high bridge that Chance had seen from the river.

"How far?"

"Thirty minutes," the man called back over his shoulder.

Did Ellen have that kind of time? Ellen started mumbling, throwing her head back and forth. She was delirious.

Guilt flooded him. Chance had never felt more helpless in his life. Here he was a doctor and he couldn't even help Ellen. He should have put her on a plane straight home the minute he'd seen her. This country and the type of work the clinic did was too dangerous. She should be someplace less demanding.

They left the city and drove along the highway into a less populated area. The hot wind coming through the open windows did nothing to make him feel more comfortable. They sped down the road but it wasn't fast enough for Chance. Houses started showing up again as they approached what he desperately hoped was San Pedro Sula.

The man pulled off the highway and made a few turns until he entered the drive of a pink sprawling building with a flat roof. Instead of stopping in front of it, he drove under the awning with the word *Emergencia* on the sign.

As the car came to a stop, Chance opened the door. He

lifted Ellen into his arms and headed for the glass doors. As he came to a desk he said, "I'm Dr. Freeman. This woman needs medical attention now."

A nurse in a white dress came toward him with concern on her face. "This way."

Chance followed her down a hallway to an exam room that looked like something out of the nineteen-fifties, but it appeared clean and adequate. Beggars couldn't be choosers and he was glad to have anything that would offer Ellen a chance to live.

He placed Ellen on the examination table. "I need a suture kit. An IV set up. Any penicillin-based medicine you have. *Stat.*" He started unlacing Ellen's boot.

The nurse stood there stunned.

A man in a white lab coat came into the room. "Who are you and what are you doing in my ER?"

"Dr. Freeman, of the Traveling Clinic. My friend needs medical attention. She has been bitten by a spider. Her fever is high. Blood pressure up and her heart rate irregular. She is dehydrated, hasn't eaten in three days and sunburned."

The doctor said something to the nurse but Chance paid no attention to their conversation.

Chance was done explaining himself. He had Ellen to see about and no one was going to prevent him from doing so. After removing her boot and sock, he asked the nurse for scissors and she handed them to him. Without hesitating, Chance started cutting away Ellen's pants leg. His lips tightened when he saw her wound. There was no way she wasn't in extreme pain.

"Help me roll her to her stomach." He didn't speak to anyone in particular but the doctor came forward to assist him. Together they settled Ellen so that Chance could see the wound clearly.

What he needed to clean the wound showed up on the

table beside Ellen. It wasn't the sterilized plastic covered prepackaged set-up he normally used but he was glad to see the instruments. Over the next hour he opened and cleaned the wound. While he was busy the nurse took care of starting an IV. As he worked, he checked to make sure it was done to his satisfaction.

Chance began preparing to bandage the wound when the Honduran doctor said, "The nurse will take care of that. It's time you tell me what's been going on and for you to be examined."

The idea of arguing with the doctor crossed Chance's mind but by the determined look on the man's face it wouldn't make a difference. "Agreed. But I need to make a phone call first."

Ellen's eyes flickered open. For once her leg wasn't screaming with pain, taking her to the point of tears. The last thing she remembered was Chance carrying her piggyback.

She looked around the room. It was a simple one with white walls and very few furnishings. A hospital room? It reminded her of the black and white pictures on the history wall of the hospital where she'd done her fellowship. Her gaze came to rest on a sleeping Chance leaning back in a chair far too small for him. Clean-shaven and dressed in clothes that were probably borrowed, he looked wonderful.

When he woke would he gather her in his arms? She wanted that. Desperately.

They were out of the jungle. Safe. He hadn't been hurt. She was alive. They had shared something special. Did he feel the same way? By all his actions he must. He had cared for her tenderly. She remembered him brushing her hair back. Speaking to her encouragingly. Begging her to hang in there until he found help.

But wouldn't he have done that for anyone? Chance was a dedicated doctor.

He'd said no promises. Had never spoken of tomorrow other than when they were going to get out of the jungle.

Chance stirred. He blinked.

"Hey." Her voice was little more than a whisper.

He sat forward. Urgency filled his voice as he asked, "How're you feeling?"

No sweetheart. She wanted to hear him say sweetheart. "Better. Thanks for saving my life."

He shrugged. "I'm just sorry you had to go through that."

Fear built, swirling around her. Why didn't he touch her? Kiss her? Had something changed? She fiddled with the hem of the bedsheet. "I think we both went through it."

"You got the worse end of things." He stood.

Why didn't he come closer? Chance walked across the small space. He looked at her.

"It couldn't have been great fun carrying me around on your back." She paused. "Tell me what happened after I passed out."

He relayed what she was sure were the highlights and little of the drama that had gone into getting her to safety. "Where are we?"

"San Pedro Sula for now." He turned and paced the other direction.

They were interrupted by a nurse entering. She spoke to Chance. "We are ready."

"Ready for what?" Ellen asked.

Now he looked at her. "I called your father. He has sent a plane for you."

Ellen sat up in bed. "You what? You had no right to make that kind of decision for me." Her head swam and she leaned back.

"You need attention that can't be given here. It's my

responsibly to see about you. You should be in a hospital in the US and checked out completely. Your body has been through a major ordeal. You need to be seen by a cardiologist."

"I don't need you to see about me. I'm a grown woman who can make her own decisions."

"Yeah, and see where that got you." He moved across the room again.

"It could have been you instead of me who was bitten."

He gave her a pointed look. "But it wasn't."

"What about you? Are you coming? You went through the same ordeal."

"The doctor here checked me out."

"But I'm feeling better." She was weak but she wouldn't admit how much.

"You've been out of your head for most of two days. You need to go home and get healthy."

"When will I see you again?" Ellen reached out a hand. She saw the hesitation in his face before he walked over and took it. His hand was large, warm and safe. She never wanted to let it go.

"I don't know for sure."

"You're running now. Just like you did when you came down here."

"What're you talking about? I'm not running anywhere."

"You're running away from me. You can't hide here forever, you know. One day you're going to have to face the fact that you have to take a gamble on someone again. We aren't all like your mother and your ex-wife. Some of us can be loyal."

He pulled his hand away. "This is not the time or the place to be having this conversation. You don't need to get upset."

Ellen wanted to snatch his hand back but he'd crammed

both in his pockets. She didn't care about anything but him. This was her heart on the line. "Okay, if we don't talk about it now, then when?"

He looked toward the wall instead of at her. "I don't know."

"See, there it is. You're shutting me out."

Chance's look met hers. He growled, "I'm not! I'm thinking about your safety. You could have been killed out there."

"I'm a big girl. I make my own decisions. Can take what comes my way."

"And down here those decisions can get people killed. Get you hurt."

"What're you trying to say?"

"That in your fight for freedom you can be reckless. Can get people hurt. Get yourself hurt. Sometimes you need to think before you act. You go all in, heart leading. No wonder your father feels the need to shelter you."

If she didn't feel so awful she'd climb out of the bed and stomp her foot. "That's not fair."

Two men that looked like orderlies entered with a squeaking gurney. She and Chance said no more as the men settled her on it. They wheeled her from the room and down the hall. Chance walked at her feet.

As they lifted her into the ambulance Chance said, "It's for your own good."

Her gaze remained locked with his as the attendants pushed the doors together. "I don't need you to protect me, I need you to love me."

The doors clicked closed. Ellen held a sob threatening to escape.

The nurse that was riding with her patted her shoulder. "The doctor must care a great deal to sit by your bed for two days and nights."

If only he would admit it.

CHAPTER NINE

CHANCE HAD BEEN miserable before. But never on this level. He missed Ellen with a vengeance. Everything that happened at the clinic reminded him of her. Each child they saw he imagined Ellen teasing a smile out of him or her. Anytime an unusual case came in he wanted to discuss it with her.

The nights were the worst. He wanted Ellen in his arms. All he had to do was look at his hammock on his porch and think of those moments they had spent there. Taking a shower became something to dread instead of something to look forward to at the end of a long hot day. It reminded him too much of standing in the falls with Ellen.

How had she managed to fill all the cracks in his life to the point he almost needed her to breathe?

His staff had taken to not asking him anything unless it was medically related. He'd given the bare minimum of information about Ellen's and his time on the run. But beyond that he didn't want to talk about the fear, guilt and relief he'd suffered through over the three days they had been in the jungle and, worse, those when she had been so sick. He certainly didn't want to discuss those intense life-changing moments when he and Ellen had made love.

Love. That had been such an elusive emotion in his life

he would have sworn he had no idea what it was. Then in had waltzed Dr. Ellen Cox. Bright smile, infallible attitude, and fortitude that could withstand the worst situation. And it had. He needed someone in his life like that, but did she need someone in hers like him?

A guy who felt he had nothing to offer her. One who chose to work in a developing country. A dangerous one. With Ellen's background, would she really be content to live and work here with him? She had seemed to love it when she was here as much as he did. Would she feel the same way after she fully recovered?

Anticipation and insecurity hit him at the same time. He'd given up on having a wife, really caring for someone, long ago. But Ellen had him thinking *Can I?* again.

She deserved someone who could sustain an ongoing relationship. He'd not ever managed to do so. Was it possible for him? History said no. Could he learn? The real question was that if he wanted Ellen, was he willing to try?

She'd been disappointed in him when she'd found out he had a sister that he didn't stay in contact with. Maybe he should start there. Would Abigail be interested in seeing him? Could they be a family after all these years? Did they even have anything in common outside being from the same dysfunctional family? Every fiber in his being said Ellen would be pleased to know he'd tried. That alone was enough reason to make an effort. But something deep inside him was screaming for him to do it for himself as well. See if he could handle a relationship.

Ellen wiped her cheek and declared she'd shed her last tear over Chance Freeman. She'd not heard anything from him in the six weeks since she had been home. Not a word.

She was cycling though the steps of grief and she was firmly on anger. As far as she was concerned, she could stay on that emotion for a long time. If she saw him now it might be dangerous for him.

Michael had called and invited her out to lunch the Saturday after Thanksgiving. She had been tickled to see him. He'd filled her in on what had been going on with the clinic and had told her a few funny stories about the patients but that was about it. She was hungry for information about Chance but the only thing Michael had said was that he would be home during the Christmas holidays.

How could Chance act this way after what they had shared in the jungle? After she had exposed her heart? Had she misjudged the type of person Chance was? Keeping the resentment at bay was difficult. Even when her mother had died she hadn't felt this abandoned. She hadn't had a choice. Chance did. If anyone should know how she was feeling it should be him. So why didn't he care enough to do something about it?

When he did come to the States, would he call her? Ask to see her? How could a man be so smart yet so dense? She clenched her teeth, almost as angry with herself for caring as she was with Chance.

That went for her father as well. He'd been harping on at her for weeks to take a job at the big teaching hospital in the city. He'd even had one of his buddies call and put in a good word for her. Today was the day that they had the talk that was long overdue.

She had given her apartment up when she'd left for Honduras so her father had insisted that she stay with him until she figured out what she was going to do next. That wasn't a question. She already knew what she was going to do. Return to Honduras, and if not there then someplace that really needed her.

Her father had had a fit when she had announced the week before that she was on the schedule at the clinic where she had worked in the city. The conversation had gone something like, you could have been killed, you are lucky to be alive, you should be grateful, you need to think about what you are doing. She didn't expect today's discussion to go much better but what she had to say needed to be said.

Chance had accused her of being reckless. She'd never thought of herself that way. Her father had put her in a box of protection that she had wanted to get out of but which had made her take chances. When her mother had died she'd learned at a young age that life was short, but had she really become irresponsible with her decisions?

The last thing she wanted to do was put anyone in danger. She knew from her and her mother's accident that poor decisions could cause horrible outcomes. Did she get so caught up in what she wanted that she didn't think about others? Had she been reckless where Chance was concerned?

She'd made reservations at her and her father's favorite café and arrived early enough that she had gotten them a table in the back. Despite the hustle and bustle of Christmas shoppers stopping for a break, they would have a quiet place to talk.

"How're you feeling?" her father asked, after he'd kissed her and taken his seat.

He was a large, burly man who looked out of place in a suit despite having worn one most of his life. Ellen liked nothing better than being pulled into one of his bear hugs. They had never had a real disagreement until she had informed him she was going to Honduras. She had not left on good terms and had returned to him telling her he'd told her so. Today's conversation wouldn't be an easy one.

"Much better. I'm not having to sit down as often at work as I did the first few days."

"You went through some ordeal. Dr. Freeman didn't

tell me a lot but from the look of you when you got to the plane you had been close to death."

Her father had come for her himself. Had even brought their private doctor with him.

The waitress came to their table for their order.

"I'll have afternoon tea," Ellen told her.

"I'll have the same," her father said. As the waitress moved away he continued, "I don't know what I would've done if I had lost you. It isn't fair to put me through something like that. Sometimes you're so like your mother."

There it was. The guilt. Had her mother really been reckless or just enjoying life? Even if Ellen was like her mother, her feelings and desires had merit. She deserved to live her own life.

"I'm sorry. Maybe I do need to be more careful but that doesn't mean I need to give up my dreams just to make you happy."

She had to make it clear she wasn't going to live in a bubble just for him. That she needed his love and support but not at the cost of what she wanted. She'd learned life was too short for that. More recently, and in the past.

"Dad, it didn't happen to you. I was the one who had the reaction to the spider bite."

"Yes, but I was the one scared to death that I might lose you."

What little she could remember about Chance after she'd become sick, he had been scared too but he had still praised her for her strength, encouraged her to keep going. He'd been concerned about her but had never wanted to hold her back. Her father wanted to do just that.

"Yeah, it was pretty frightening in parts. But I'm here."

"And that's where I want you to stay."

"That's what I want to talk to you about."

His bushy brows rose.

"Daddy, I'm going back to Honduras if the clinic will

have me. If not, then I'll go to another Central American country to work."

Her father's palm slapped on the table, rattling the silverware. "Haven't you had enough? After what happened to you?"

"Daddy, I know you love me. I know I'm all you have. But this is something I'm compelled to do. I'm grown, heaven's sake I'm a doctor. I'm needed there. I wished you would understand but if you don't, that is fine. I have to go anyway."

Her father studied her. "Does this have something to do with Dr. Freeman?"

She looked away. "Some, but not all."

"That's what I thought. I had him checked out. He's known for having women falling for him."

Her chest tightened. She could understand why. She certainly had. "That may be so but that doesn't mean he doesn't do good work. That the Traveling Clinic doesn't have value."

"There's plenty of work you can do here. Of value. Did you even talk to the hospital about the job?"

"Daddy, I'm not going to. That's not where I belong."

The waitress returned with their tea. They sat quietly until she had finished placing the tea stand in front of them and left.

"I love you, Daddy. I do, but I have to be true to myself. I know you have lost. I have too. I miss Mother every day. I know you worry about me. You've worked to protect me. But you can't do that forever. I'll get hurt. Bad things will happen to me. That's life. What I need is your support. Encouragement."

Her father ate without saying anything. He finally looked at her. His eyes glistened. The last time she'd seen him close to tears had been when he'd sat beside her bed in the hospital and had had to tell her that her mother had died.

"I love you dearly. The only thing I've ever wanted to do was keep you safe. See that you were cared for."

"You have."

"I do support you. Want the best for you, but you can't stop me from worrying about you."

She placed her hand on his arm. "I know and I love you for it."

For the rest of their time together they talked about their plans for Christmas and what gifts they might like to receive. They were pulling on their coats to go out into the snowy weather when Ellen asked, "Dad, have you ever thought about dating? You're still a young man."

Those brows of his rose again. "What brought that on?"

She tugged at his lapel, lifting in around his neck. "I just think that everyone should share their life with someone who cares about them. You've concentrated on me long enough. It's time for you to live."

"Have you found someone you want to share your life with?"

"I thought I had."

Her father kissed her forehead and tucked her arm though his. "One thing I've learned in this life is that anything can happen."

Did she dare hope?

She returned to her father's penthouse to prepare for her shift at the clinic that evening. An envelope lay waiting on the table in the hall with her name on it. Inside was an invitation to a gala event to benefit the Honduras Traveling Clinic.

Would Chance attend? Did she care if he did?

Chance had been in the States a week. There had been meetings at the foundation and a couple of speaking engagements. Ellen constantly called to him. If he went to her would she even speak to him after so much time had passed? She had to be mad. He couldn't blame her.

He'd kept tabs on how she was doing. Once he had called and spoken to her father. Not known for being easily intimidated, Chance's conversation with Mr. Cox had been an uneasy one. He was a man who loved his daughter deeply and Chance had put her in danger. It wasn't something her father was going to forgive quickly. Their discussion had been to the point but Chance had learned what his heart so desperately wanted to know. Ellen was doing well. Had recovered. For that Chance would be forever grateful.

He also checked up on her through Michael. He had seen her at Thanksgiving and Chance was jealous. What he wouldn't give to just see her for a second. Make sure for himself she was fine.

When Michael had returned he'd had enough compassion for Chance that he hadn't made him ask about Ellen. Michael had offered right off that he'd had lunch with Ellen.

"She's back at work at the same inner-city clinic she was at before she came down here." Michael had spoken to everyone at the dinner table but had given Chance a pointed look. "Says she coming back here or another Central American country as soon as the doctor gives her a complete release. Which should be soon."

Karen spoke up. "We sure could use her here."

In more ways than one. Chance ached with the need to touch her, hold her. See her smile.

"You should talk to her when we you go to the States next week, Chance. Get her to consider coming back here," Pete added.

"Yes, you should speak to her," Michael stated. "She asked how everyone is doing."

Michael looked at him again. There was a deeper meaning to his words, he was sure.

Would Ellen really want to see him? He'd done the one thing that could destroy her trust.

Called her father. She'd said she wanted his love. Could he give it? Take a chance on her leaving him? Maybe she had changed her mind. After all, their relationship had been during a fight for life. They'd been emotionally strung out. Had what she'd said about wanting love been in the heat of the moment?

What Ellen had done was make him determined to contact his sister. See if he could repair that bridge. He'd put off seeing her long enough. Gripping the phone with a knot in his throat, he remembered what they'd said to each other at their father's funeral. She'd invited him to their father's house for the will reading. Chance had had no interest in ever going there again. He'd told her she could have the house and everything else, that he only wanted the cabin. It was about two hours away and gave him a home base when he was in country.

"But you'll keep in touch, won't you? I would like to know how you are doing."

Chance had just nodded, making no commitment. She'd called him a few times but when he'd not returned them the calls had become fewer then died away. His sister had left him too. Or was it more like he'd pushed her way? Had he done the same with Ellen?

The phone rang almost long enough that Chance thought he had a reprieve. Just as he was preparing to hang up a woman answered.

"May I speak to Abigail? Tell her it's Chance."

"Chance?" The sound of disbelief had him regretting so many things he'd left undone and unsaid.

"Abigail?"

"Yes."

"I'm in town until after the Christmas holidays and I was wondering if you would like to have lunch?"

The pause was so long that he was afraid she might have hung up. Then there was a sniffle on the other end of the line. "Why don't you come here for dinner? Tomorrow night at six."

"Okay, I'll be there."

Chance drove up the drive to the large Tudor-style home built among the trees in an affluent neighborhood. This was his childhood home. There were few happy memories here for him.

He stood outside the front door for a minute before he knocked. As if she was standing behind it, waiting for him, the door opened and Abigail reached out and took him in her arms. "It's about time, Chance-man."

That had been her nickname for him growing up. He forgotten about it.

"It's about time." Now she was using that big-sister reprimand voice.

"I know. I should have come before."

She pulled him into the house and closed the door. Her husband and children waited in the hall. The excitement in her voice couldn't be denied. "Stan, Chance is here. Wendy and Jonathan."

Chance was caught up in a whirlwind of hugs and hellos. What had he missed all these years?

Dinner was served in the same room where dinner had been served when his father had come home but this time it wasn't a meeting of a family that was unsure of each other but of one glad to see each other. Chance hadn't enjoyed a meal more since Ellen had left.

To his great surprise, his sister knew about his work and the family had numerous questions about the Travelling Clinic and Honduras. The discussion was open and frank, with none of the tension he'd expected.

As the kitchen help began clearing the table, Abigail suggested they have coffee in the other room. The living room was the same place but the furniture had been replaced with a more modern version. What really held Chance's attention were the pictures. They were of the smiling and happy group of people who now lived in the house. There were even a couple of pictures of him and Abigail as children. Here he had been part of a family and hadn't even known it. Abigail had not abandoned him.

Her husband and children joined them for a while but slowly drifted away as if they were giving him and Abigail a chance to talk.

"Chance, I'm so glad you are here. I have missed you."

"I've missed you too." To his amazement he meant it.

"I'm sorry we've been so distant for so long. I wished it had been different."

He did too, but couldn't admit it out loud.

"I should have done better as the older sister in keeping in touch. I shouldn't have given up. You are my family."

She had cared. Abigail had carried a burden as well. "There wasn't anything you could have done. That was on me."

"When you came home from school at Christmas you were so different. I couldn't seem to reach you any more. After Daddy died you just never came around again. It was like you blamed me as well as Dad for sending you away."

He had. His mother had been gone. His father hadn't wanted him and his sister had said she couldn't take him. There had been nothing secure in his life and he'd wanted nothing to do with her betrayal.

"I wish I could have made it different for you. Fixed it so you could stay with me, but Daddy would have none of it. He said I was too young to see about you and that you were going to learn to behave. That sending you off to school was the way to do it. I fought for you but he wouldn't let you stay."

All this time Chance had believed she hadn't wanted him around. Had blamed her.

"Those weren't happy years for me either and I know they weren't for you. I hated that we were separated. I hated more that you wanted nothing to do with me. After a while I didn't know how to bridge the gap. Then you wouldn't let me and I stopped trying."

"Part of that is my fault."

"Then let's just start here and go forward. Promise me we'll see each other often. After all, we are family."

Family. That sounded good. "You have my word."

"We'll see you at Christmas." It wasn't a question but a statement.

"I'll be here."

"Chance, you may not want to talk about this but I just want to let you know that I saved your half of the inheritance for you. It's been in the bank, waiting on you."

He would never have thought he would be interested in the money but he knew where he could put it to good use. "Thank you."

"You're welcome. I would've never felt right about keeping it."

After his evening with Abigail and her family Chance saw his past and his sister in a different light. Had he been unjust in his view of Ellen too?

Could he humble himself and beg enough to convince her he loved her and would never let her go again? He could if that was what it took to rid himself of the unceasing ache for her.

CHAPTER TEN

CHANCE PULLED AT his tux jacket. He didn't make a habit of dressing up in one and he knew why. They were uncomfortable. Here it was a week before Christmas and he was going to some fancy party. He much preferred a T-shirt and cargo shorts.

He wasn't fond of a dog-and-pony show but he'd participate in the gala if that was what it took to raise money for the clinic. Tonight's event in the great hall of the Metropolitan Museum of Art, if successful, should raise enough money to supply the clinic for the next year and give him start-up funds for a permanent building.

What he really wanted to do was find Ellen and beg her to forgive him for being such an idiot. If his sister could welcome him back, maybe Ellen could too. He had a feeling he would have to work harder where Ellen was concerned.

From wealthy and socially known families on both sides, maiden and married, his sister was well connected. To Chance's shock she'd been on a committee that helped fundraise for the clinic for years. Abby's group had already had this event planned before he'd called her. She'd asked him to attend and say a few words about his work in Honduras.

The great hall of the Met was already crowded with

guests and more were arriving by the time Chance made it there.

"Doesn't the place look beautiful with all the twinkling lights and the Christmas tree?" his sister said beside him after they had left her wrap and the men's overcoats at the cloakroom.

Chance was sure he would have been overwhelmed by the event if it hadn't been for his social training during boarding school. He certainly didn't attend anything like this in Honduras.

Was Ellen here? If she wasn't, he would leave to find her. Chance didn't see her in the crush of people. He'd had his sister send her and her father an invitation. It wouldn't be like Ellen not to show up. Despite how she might feel about him, she would be supportive of the clinic. In this environment, he hoped she might be more favorable to listening to him plead for her forgiveness.

A woman who Abigail whispered to him was the head of the fund-raising committee took the stage and asked for the crowd's attention. She thanked everyone for coming and introduced him, requesting he come forward.

As he spoke he scanned the room. *Was she there?* Once he thought he saw Ellen but if it was her she'd moved out of sight. He gave his prepared speech, which included sharing about how a visiting doctor had communicated with young girls over fingernail polish, pointing out that the smallest things could make a big difference. Ellen had taught him that. That the work wasn't just about the grand scale but the small everyday efforts and relationships the clinic was building.

When he had finished, the committee chair returned to the stage. "We have a little something different planned for this evening. We're going to have the men make a pledge of support in order to dance the first dance with a woman of their choice. Would anyone like to start the pledging?"

There was a soft murmur around the room then a man in the middle of the crowd raised his hand. "I bid a thousand dollars for a dance with my wife."

"Come on, is that all Margaret is worth?" the committee chair said with a smile. "You can do better than that, Henry."

"Make it five, then," the man called.

"That's better. Please come up and sign your pledge card and escort your partner to the dance floor. Anyone else? Come on, gentlemen, what's a dance worth to you?"

"I bid five thousand dollars for a dance with Miss Jena Marshall," called a young man.

"I bid six for the same lady," another man said.

"Make that seven," the first man came back.

The chairwoman looked at the other man but he shook his head. With a smile she said, "Miss Marshall, I believe you have your partner."

From Chance's vantage point beside the stage he could see the smile on the girl's face. While the committee chair was encouraging another bid, he caught a glimpse of Ellen. A joy so large filled him to the point he didn't know if his chest could contain it.

"I bid ten thousand dollars for a dance with Ellen Cox," said a man Chance couldn't see.

Without hesitation Chance lifted his hand. "I bid fifty thousand dollars for a dance with Dr. Cox."

Heat swept over Ellen. Her heart did a fast tap dance and she stood stock still. A hush had fallen over the crowd and everyone looked toward her.

She knew that voice. It called to her in her dreams. The voice she hadn't heard in weeks until tonight.

Her body had jerked and flushed when Chance's name

had been called to come to the stage just half an hour earlier. Her traitorous heart had flipped. *He's here!*

Why hadn't Chance gotten in touch with her? *Because he doesn't care.* After so many weeks of not hearing from him that could only be the answer. Despite that, his informative speech, which was filled with knowledge and passion for what he did, had her falling in love with Honduras and him all over again.

She stood glued to the floor until someone nudged her forward. The crowd separated as she moved to meet him on shaky legs. Chance's bid made her feel dizzy. Why did he want to dance with her? He could have given the money to the clinic without involving her. Where had he gotten that kind of money?

Ellen had smiled when the interesting pledge twist had been announced. It could either be a flop or a hit. Ellen had been interested to see which. She had watched as her father had made his way to the front of the room. His amazing bid had blown her away. He knew how important the clinic was to her, even if he didn't support her working there.

Now Chance stood in front of her. He was so handsome in his tux it almost hurt to look at him.

A flutter of excitement filled her midsection. She had to remind herself of how angry she was. So why was she so pleased to see him?

The band played the first notes of a waltz.

Chance offered his hand. "May I have this dance?"

She said in a low voice, "I don't want to."

There was a surprised gasp from a few people around them.

He met and held her gaze. "Sweetheart, I'm sorry."

"Don't call me that," she hissed. "It's been almost two months since I've spoken to you."

His smile never wavered. "Let's not fight about it here. We can find someplace private to talk after our dance."

Ellen heard the pleading in his voice and took his hand. It was like coming home to touch him again. He led her to the dance floor and there his arm came to rest at her waist. She could hardly breathe. Her hands shook. She worked to push the pure happiness down, to stop it from overflowing and washing her anger away. They moved across the floor. Chance was an excellent dancer. But even if he hadn't been, she was in heaven by just being in his arms again.

You are mad at him. Remember that.

"I've missed you."

Could she trust him? Was he playing at something? She'd already spent two months in misery. Her feet quit moving. "You think you can literally waltz in here after not speaking to me for weeks and I'm going to fall at your feet?"

"No, that's the last thing I thought. With you I was fully anticipating I'd have to fight my way back into your good graces." He pulled her closer.

Ellen pushed against his shoulder, putting some space between them. "Just where did you get fifty thousand dollars?"

"Let's just say I came into some money. By the way, you look beautiful. That green is gorgeous on you."

She couldn't help but warm at his praise.

"How're you feeling? How's your leg doing?"

"Now you're showing interest?" She wasn't going to give him the chance to hurt her further.

He didn't ease his hold as he whispered close to her ear, "I've always been interested."

"You have a funny way of showing it. No phone calls. No handwritten letter. Not even an email or text."

He twirled her away from him and then brought her back to his chest. "I deserve that. And more. But I have checked on you."

She glared at him. "When?"

"I spoke to your father after you'd been back in the States a couple of days. And Michael gave me a report."

"At least *he* cared enough to see me when he was here."

"I'm sorry. I should have called you. I have no excuse but that I was a coward. I screwed up."

"Well, you're right about that."

He lowered his voice and searched her face. "How are you?"

"Do you really want to know?"

"Yes, I want to know everything about you. I've missed you."

"I'm fine. I've been back to work for a number of weeks. The leg is healing nicely." She purposely filled her voice with sarcasm. "I had a good doctor."

"Yeah, but not much of a human being."

"You expect me to disagree with that?"

"I really am sorry. If you'll forgive me I'll spend the rest of my life trying to make it up to you."

Hope soared within her. What did he mean by the rest of his life?

The number ended and Chance released her from his arms but continued to hold her hand. "I'd like you to meet my sister and her husband."

"What?" So he had contacted his sister. She was so surprised she didn't stop him from leading her off the dance floor.

He grinned. "You sure are using that word a lot. I've never known you to be at a loss for words."

Leading her to a group of people standing near the refreshment table, he waited until a couple broke away.

"Abigail and Stan, I'd like you to meet Dr. Ellen Cox," Chance said. "She worked at the clinic for a while. I'm hoping to convince her to return."

Ellen's eyes widened. She stared at him. Chance wanted her to return?

"It's so nice to meet you, Ellen. We appreciate all the work you have done. I know Chance will be glad to have you join him again." His sister's smile was sincere.

Ellen's head was spinning with all that Chance had said. She hoped she made all the proper responses to Chance's sister's remarks. Had she walked into a third dimension where everyone understood what was happening but her?

Chance broke in on the conversation and said to his sister, "If it's okay with Ellen, I'm going to take her somewhere so we can talk privately. I'll see you at the hotel tomorrow."

Abigail nodded.

He kept a hand on Ellen's waist as they sidestepped their way toward the cloakroom.

"Why do you think I want to talk to you?" Ellen asked.

"Don't you?" He kept her moving, not giving her time to argue.

A number of times people stopped them to ask him a question or make a comment. Keeping a hand on Ellen, he smiled and gave a short answer then made an excuse to move on.

"I think what you haven't said in the last few weeks speaks loudly enough."

He handed their tickets to the attendant and collected their coats.

"Please, let me explain."

The clerk handed him Ellen's full-length hooded cape, with white fur inside and the same green as her dress on the outside, edged with fluffy fur. He placed it over her shoulders.

"You look like a Christmas fairy." Chance was mesmerized. "I thought you were beautiful before but you take my breath away."

"Not too over the top?" She made a half-twirl.

It was the first really civil thing she had said to him all night. She was coming around slowly. "You're amazing."

She smiled at him. His heart flipped. He was headed in the right direction. Pulling on his overcoat, he beamed back at her. "I have missed you."

Bundled up, they stepped through the outside doors into a snowy night.

"It's beautiful." Ellen looked up into the sky illuminated by the lights of the skyscrapers. "I love this city at Christmastime."

Chance offered his elbow as they made their way down the numerous steps to the street. "It's completely different from Honduras."

"Which is equally beautiful in its own way." She took his arm but he was sure it was more out of the need for help than her having forgiven him. Ellen wouldn't go easy on him. He had hurt her deeply. They continued downward. "Where're we going?" she asked.

"How about a carriage ride?"

"Now you're turning into Mr. Romance?"

"That's my Ellen. Give no quarter."

"I'm not yours."

He needed to slow down. Give her time to think. Stopping, he looked at her a second. "Maybe not, but I'm hoping you will be. Just hear me out, please."

She nodded and he led her to a horse-drawn carriage parked on the street. It was decked out in white lights and bells for the season. He spoke to the driver and then helped Ellen into the carriage. With her settled in the seat, Chance joined her and pulled the heavy blanket waiting there across their waists and legs, tucking it around them.

"Warm?" he asked.

"Mmm…"

The horse started off at a slow clop-clop and continued as they turned into Central Park. The jingle of the bells on the horse's rig only added to the perfect winter dream feel of the moment.

"It's been forever since I've taken a ride through the park. I've never done it in the dark while it's snowing." She raised her face to the sky. "I love the sound of the bells. It's magical."

"Sort of like standing under a waterfall," he said softly.

"Yeah. Just like that." Wonder filled her voice.

She was softening. He took her hand under the blanket.

Her eyes came around to pierce him with a look. This was the Ellen he knew so well. "Why haven't you called?"

There it was. The hurt. Raw and deep.

"Because I didn't want to face what I feel."

She continued to glare at him. "I like that answer."

He brushed a snowflake from her cheek. "I thought you might. I'm sorry, Ellen. I was an idiot. There hasn't been a moment I haven't thought of you."

"You had a fine way of showing it."

"I know. You made me think about caring for someone again. But that brought the fear of rejection. I had to face my past before I could ask you about a future."

"So you reached out to your sister?"

Chance nodded. Ellen squeezed his hand. It was as if that one action had shown her that he meant what he was saying.

"I'm so proud of you. That couldn't have been easy."

"You know that if you had died it would have killed me."

Ellen pulled her hand from his and cupped his cheek. Her hand was warm against his cold skin. "I'm made of tougher stuff than you give me credit for."

He covered her hand with his. "I know that now. You have more than proved it. I love you, sweetheart."

A smile spread across her face. "That's all I've ever wanted. I love you too."

He held her close and kissed her. Her lips were cold against his but they soon warmed.

"I told my father I was returning to Honduras or another developing country," Ellen said, with her head against his shoulder.

"How did he take that?"

"Better than I thought he would. He still wants to protect me but he is also starting to understand my need for independence. This time he knows I'm not rushing into a decision."

"No more being reckless?" Chance asked.

"I promise to think twice before I react."

"And I promise to let you be who you are without holding you back."

She gifted him with a bright smile. "I love you, Chance Freeman. I also promise to never leave you."

His hands cupped her cheeks and kissed her softly with all the love in his heart. "If you tried, I would come and find you. I love you."

Chance had found what had been missing in his life. It was all right here in his arms.

* * * * *

If you enjoyed this story, check out these other great reads from Susan Carlisle

MARRIED FOR THE BOSS'S BABY
ONE NIGHT BEFORE CHRISTMAS
HIS BEST FRIEND'S BABY
THE DOCTOR'S REDEMPTION

All available now!

MILLS & BOON®

EXCLUSIVE EXTRACT

Saoirse Murphy's proposal of a 'convenient'
arrangement with paramedic Santiago Valentino
soon ignites a very inconvenient passion...

Read on for a sneak preview of
SANTIAGO'S CONVENIENT FIANCÉE
by Annie O'Neil

Saoirse went up on tiptoe and kissed him.

From the moment her lips touched Santiago's she
didn't have a single lucid thought. Her brain all but
exploded in a vain attempt to unravel the quick-fire
sensations. Heat, passion, need, longing, sweet and tangy
all jumbled together in one beautiful confirmation that
his lips were every bit as kissable as she'd thought they
might be.

Snippets of what was actually happening were hitting
her in blips of delayed replay.

Her fingers tangled in his silky, soft hair. Santi's wide
hands tugged her in tight, right at the small of her back.
There was no doubting his body's response to her now.
The heated pleasure she felt when one of his hands
slipped under her T-shirt elicited an undiluted moan of
pleasure. He matched her move for move as if they had
been made for one another. Her body's reaction to his
felt akin to hitting all hundred watts her body was capable
of for the very first time.

She wanted more.

No.

She wanted it *all*. The whole package. The feelings. The pitter-patter of her heart. Knowing it was reciprocated. Being part of a shared love. Not some sham wedding so she wouldn't have to live in a country where her soul had all but shriveled up and died.

She felt Santi's kisses deepen and her will-power to shore up some sort of resistance to what was happening plummeted. This felt so *real*. And a little too close to everything she'd hoped for wrapped up in a too-good-to-be-true package. That sort of thing didn't happen to her. And it wasn't. She'd started it, Santi was just responding. She heard herself moan and with its escape her resolve to resist abandoned her completely.

Don't miss
SANTIAGO'S CONVENIENT FIANCÉE
by Annie O'Neill

Available January 2017
www.millsandboon.co.uk

MILLS & BOON®

Why shop at millsandboon.co.uk?

Each year, thousands of romance readers find their perfect read at millsandboon.co.uk. That's because we're passionate about bringing you the very best romantic fiction. Here are some of the advantages of shopping at www.millsandboon.co.uk:

* **Get new books first**—you'll be able to buy your favourite books one month before they hit the shops

* **Get exclusive discounts**—you'll also be able to buy our specially created monthly collections, with up to 50% off the RRP

* **Find your favourite authors**—latest news, interviews and new releases for all your favourite authors and series on our website, plus ideas for what to try next

* **Join in**—once you've bought your favourite books, don't forget to register with us to rate, review and join in the discussions

Visit **www.millsandboon.co.uk**
for all this and more today!